DRAGONFLIES

ALSO BY GRANT BUDAY

Rootbound, ECW Press, 2006

A Sack of Teeth, Raincoast Books, 2002

Golden Goa, ECW Press, 2000

White Lung, Anvil Press, 1999

Dragonflies

Grant Buday

BIBLIOASIS

FIRST EDITION

Library and Archives Canada Cataloguing in Publication

Buday, Grant, 1956–
        Dragonflies / Grant Buday.

ISBN 10: 1-897231-47-4
ISBN 13: 978-1-897231-47-0

        I. Title.
PS8553.U444D73 2008   C813'.54   C2008-904361-8

Cover iStockphoto: "Ancient Greek Corinthian Helmet"
        © Keith Binns.

Edited by Daniel Wells.

**Canada Council   Conseil des Arts
for the Arts   du Canada**

**ONTARIO ARTS COUNCIL
CONSEIL DES ARTS DE L'ONTARIO**

We gratefully acknowledge the support of the Canada Council
for the Arts and the Ontario Arts Council for our publishing
program.

Though masquerading as an epic, the *Odyssey* is the first Greek novel; and therefore wholly irresponsible where myths are concerned.

—ROBERT GRAVES

Chapter One

THE WALLS OF TROY throb in the sun, a trick of the heat radiating off the limestone. Ten years I've studied those walls. Ten years. Sometimes they advance and sometimes they recede, at other times they waver and sway as if viewed through fire, at sunset their colour deepens, becoming richer, while in the rain they turn grey. In many places they are black from the burning pitch the Trojans pour down to drive us off. Each spring grass sprouts in the seams between the stones and the goats stand up on their hind legs to reach it. The walls are as high as five men. At the top there are oak palings battered by our catapults and charred from our burning arrows. In the early days the Trojans would stand there and wave to us as they pissed.

It's spring, the time of dragonflies. They're admirable hunters, patrolling the meadows, hovering, darting, killing. It's a dangerous season for men as well, for the jackals and wolves are on the move, and when we venture inland we wrap our ankles in leather against snakes. The days grow hot, the mosquito breeds, and the season of fever is near.

Soon the meadows will dry and crack and the winds from the east will carry red dust.

I'd genuinely believed we'd be home before winter. The Trojans had other ideas, laughing at our attempts to negotiate—*keep the gold but return Helen*—then catapulting goatskins loaded with rocks and scorpions at us. Soon that first summer ebbed into autumn, the leaves fell and the trees were bare. Under-supplied, we hunkered in our tents eating the last of our salted meat and drinking rainwater. I suggested returning in the spring. Agamemnon said no, he'd lose half the army and knew it.

He urged me to rally the men. *Explain that it's better this way. They'll be home sooner.*

I dutifully tried to convince the men and they dutifully tried to believe me.

Another spring and summer passed. All too soon the leaves were on the ground again and winter was back. Our breath was cold smoke and each dawn we broke discs of ice on the water pots. By the third year resentment turned to sorrow and finally to acceptance tainted by hatred. Everyone believed—though few were bold enough to say—that it was Menelaus's fault.

Menelaus still believes Helen loves him—we're not only righting a wrong, but punishing a crime and reclaiming honour. He's a king, Agamemnon's brother, and Agamemnon is also a king, and such men expect to get their way. What I want is to go home. To see my son. To see my wife. Yet Menelaus is adamant. He wants his woman and Agamemnon wants Troy, which will make him king of kings, so we've stayed. Reluctantly, doggedly. We've dug in while Agamemnon has ranted about pride, first trying to shame us and then to inspire us. The fourth summer was a bad one for fever, and then came the bloody flux, the men groaning over their red stool. Many deserted, though where they went was a mystery. Some were so desperate they reappeared months later, starved, sick, telling tales of abduction and escape. The wheels of the seasons ground past, time turning stone to sand, young men to old, black hair grey. Six years. Seven. To acceptance and hatred add contempt. What kind of man lets another one take his woman? What kind of man leaves a foreigner, a Trojan, unwatched in his home? Menelaus is an idiot and we are paying the price.

Forget Helen and the Trojan gold, the gilded doors and bronze horses, forget the pearls, the sapphires, the silk, the opium, and the reputation. Forget it all. But Agamemnon and Menelaus don't want to forget; forgetting is an art that is beyond them, in their view akin to cowardice (you see how narrowly their minds flow). They don't approve of shrewd avoidance, in my estimation as valuable a craft as that of the metal smith or the shipwright, and one not as easily mastered.

So what to do? Years of siege had failed to break the walls of Troy. We retrieved the bow and arrows of God-like Heracles, but still failed to break the walls of Troy. And then Agamemnon committed his biggest blunder of all and took Briseis from Achilles, and all too soon Achilles was dead and our last hope shrivelled with our greatest warrior on his pyre. Our world was reduced to ash, the air stank of smoke, for days we heard nothing but the cawing of ravens. Surely some god was against us. Many gods. Every imaginable sacrifice was made, thigh bones wrapped in fat, goblets of ram's blood, owl skulls, the wings of hawks. If I have contempt for Menelaus, I hate Agamemnon. He knows what he's done and that he's to blame. So what does he do, this wise king, this great man, this leader of leaders? He decides that it's up to me, Odysseus, to break the walls of Troy —when their bright swords bend and bull-hide shields split it's always up to me. They resent this. They won't say so but they do, because they don't trust me. They say I deny the gods, that I ask too many questions, that I'm out for number one, (as if they apply their minds to higher things while I, venal and greedy, talk in circles), worst of all they fear that I'll call black white—and here's what really enrages them—that I'll convince them black *is* white. For all that they celebrate a sleek argument they think there's too much of the eel in mine. But now our backs are to the sea. What choice do they have? Menelaus wants his woman and Agamemnon Troy.

*

And so the brothers pay me an official visit. I could pitch a rock from my tent to theirs, nonetheless they insist upon arriving in their tasselled chariots, sporting their lion skins, their plumes. Agamemnon has his golden staff said, by him, to have come from Zeus Cloudsplitter himself. His upper lip is freshly shaved though his lead-coloured eyes are pouched in purple. The seams caused by his brooding run deep across his brow. A leader of unshakable purpose and will, I'll give him that, but he's in decline. He's forty-seven, an old man, thick-necked and hairy, and looks nothing at all like the busts which flank the entrance to his tent, the inside of which stinks like a chicken yard.

The years have been even crueller to Menelaus. He's smaller than Agamemnon, and his shoulders, always narrow, have shrunk further. He's lost all of his lower teeth. A palsy twitches in his right hand so that he hides it behind his back. Failing eyesight makes him thrust his face forward and squint, and as for his once dazzling red hair, he now hennas it every week to hide the grey. Then there are his perpetually chapped lips. What a contrast to Paris who, though a swindler and a coward, with no more nobility than a dungheap dog, is still handsome, with a young man's clear eyes and flat gut. Ten years ago Paris arrived in Sparta wearing an indigo robe trimmed with pearls, crocodile sandals with gold clasps, his hair perfect, while all Helen had to look forward to was cotton dyed in onion skin. So off she went, taking half the treasury with her.

Menelaus and Agamemnon make their appearance just as young Sinon is plucking my ear hairs. (I ask you, why do I need hair in my ears?) I stand to greet them and we bandy the praise and usual bunk, the sort of blather I've come to despise almost as much as the brothers themselves.

"Bold Odysseus," begins Agamemnon, as if standing on a box. "Son of Laertes, grandson of Autolycus, who, with

Diomedes, stole into the Trojan camp and slew the Thracians and routed their horses, I, Agamemnon, son of Atreus, grandson of Pelops, great grandson of Tantalus, call upon you once again, for we grow weary of this war. Ten years have passed. It is time for final action." And on and on. His broken nose lends timbre to his voice, as if he speaks through a pipe. A man untroubled by self-doubt, Agamemnon regards his own piss as gold and you should be honoured to have a sip. "Think of some plan, Odysseus. Succeed where main force has failed, bend your wits to this and never shall you be absent from our feast table." He grows nobler by the minute while Menelaus stands half a step behind, squinting and twitching. Agamemnon winds it all up by saying I may state my reward. "Name it, Odysseus, name it." He gestures grandly, as though the world is his to give.

But what reward can compensate for the ten years I've lost? Chopping ten years from his life? Putting a spear up his ass? A futile line of thought, one I indulge too much. I bow in acknowledgement of such a grand offer from so eminent a lord, of course it's less an offer than a demand, for you don't disappoint the unforgiving Agamemnon. He uses men like hammers, and keeps using them until they break, and then drops them. Still, I can't deny that it *would* be a shame to stumble home empty-handed after so many years, like my father did, so I give him my thousand-mile stare and think it over, just to make him squirm, just to make him value my response, just to stake some territory. I turn and look at our beached ships parching in the sun, the eyes on the hulls overdue for repainting, the sails rotten, the woodworms relentless. Beyond them lies Tenedos and beyond that the open sea and home. "Agamemnon," I say, turning to face him at last. "King of Mycenae, Lion of the Achaeans. I'll name my reward when we are standing inside Troy, when Priam is on his knees, Paris dead, and Helen with her rightful husband, for only then will I be worthy of it."

Pleased with my response, he stands taller, though narrows his eyes as he checks my words for hidden meaning (for he is quite right that a bargain is being negotiated). "So you'll take up the task?"

"Of course."

"Good. Excellent." His hearty tone says that we are still comrades.

"The gods willing," I caution.

He inclines his head meaning he understands perfectly. "We're down to the last bulls," he adds.

I acknowledge that sacrifices are at a premium. "But can you think of a greater need?"

"None, none."

And so I send them off with praise and assurances and then call Sinon back to finish my other ear. For a time he works in silence, probing and plucking, showing me each faded auburn hair as he uproots it, every pinprick sting strangely satisfying. Hair, it sprouts all year-round, summer or winter, more relentless than grass, yet why is it that a dog's fur grows only so long and then stops? Why does my beard grow and grow while the hair on my chest stays one length?

"What will you do?" asks Sinon, interrupting these profound cogitations.

"What do you advise?" Sinon is young but has an agile and entertaining mind, and I never ignore a shrewd opinion.

He clears his throat and strikes a dignified pose. His face takes on the gravity of a king, the stern brow, the pursed lips, the elevated chin. In a chest-deep voice that is a perfect imitation of Agamemnon, he states, "Succeed, good Odysseus, and the ode masters will sing of you. For a man there can be no greater glory."

I applaud.

He bows. On a roll now, eager to perform, eager to please, he asks, "Should I do Menelaus?"

"Yes. Give me Menelaus."

Prudently glancing around in case we're being observed, he narrows his shoulders, hunches his back, takes on the pained squint of a man with weak eyes. He clenches his fists and in a cuckold's agony moans that Helen belongs to him, that she did not run away, she was kidnapped, and she loves him. "*She does. She must!*"

*

Everything falls still in the afternoon heat, the dogs sleep, the ravens go silent, the flies rest, even the waves seem to grow sluggish. The day in its lull. The breeze drops and only the sun continues to burn. The ever-attentive Sinon rolls up the walls of my tent so that it doesn't get too hot. The tent is ox hide and years of sun and wind and salt have bleached it the grey of driftwood. My single bed is a sorry sight compared to the one I built for Penelope and me with its olive tree corner post. A clever bit of joinery, the pieces fitting as perfectly as we fit each other. How charmed she was, how her eyes gleamed at the idea of a live tree imparting its spirit to our nights. I sit down and ease my feet out of my sandals, roll two wads of wax until they're pliable and then press them into my ears. This taste for seclusion is a quirk that causes suspicion; the others sleep in groups, in twos and threes. I lay down and shut my eyes and begin my afternoon ritual conjuring of Penelope. First, I recall her sea-green eyes, deep and lucid and as full of surprises as the ocean itself, then I move on to her mouth, and then to her hair, thick and black, and then her voice; there's a resonance to her voice, a small richness: if oak could sing it would be in the voice of Penelope. She likes to laugh. She enjoys people and their odd ways, is intrigued by wanderers and eccentrics. That I like the taste of burnt sulphur bemuses her, as does the fact that wind unnerves me, a sailor, and that I can hold my breath for two hundred heartbeats. Once I've conjured her face and her voice, I move down to her shoulders, to the delicate valleys behind her collarbones, then to her breasts, her navel, the slope of her hip, and then glide down to that warm and hidden place where I linger as long as I can. Later, sated, our limbs twined, she tells me how life proceeds on our farm, the weight of the eggs, the quality of the goats' milk, the state of the orange trees, the days of rain versus the days of sun. And of course all about Telemachus, how big he's grown, how much he eats, the beauty of his eyes, his capacity for numbers (no trait of mine), his imagination, and the long conversations he has with the dog, Argos. Telemachus is fourteen years old now and must be well along in his lessons in the sword and the bow. It hurts not to be there teaching him these things, that he learns them from someone else, a stranger. Worse, that he knows this other man better than he knows me, and is likely growing closer to him every day, and that when I return—if I return—we'll be as formal as if we'd never met. And all of this I blame on Menelaus.

It was summer ten years ago when word reached us that Helen had run off with Paris. A tasty bit of gossip, savoury as spitted lamb. Penelope wasn't surprised. She said it was typical, if more brazen, than Helen's previous romps. We were harvesting oranges at the time.

"Poor Tyndareus," she said. "When Helen was growing up she nearly drove him insane."

She stood atop the ladder picking oranges and passing them down. Telemachus, four years old, was swatting at the wasps with a stick while the slaves worked the other trees. "Tyndareus?" I said. "What about Menelaus?"

"Menelaus? He had a choice. He should've known what he was getting involved with. You did, didn't you?" She arched an eyebrow and regarded me. A barbed question.

"Yes," I answered quickly. "It was obvious."

That wasn't quite a lie. Nearly nine years earlier I'd gone to Sparta where all the others, Menelaus, Diomedes, Palamedes, Ajax, were competing for Helen. I was twenty and an idiot, but even I soon saw that it was all theatre and that the majestic Helen would be more curse than prize.

"The spark of Zeus runs through her," I said now, unable to resist a little teasing. "Perhaps she can't help it. Blame the gods."

Penelope aimed an orange at my head. I caught it in my basket, but now Helen was in both our thoughts. Penelope frowned and plucked angrily at the fruit causing a shower of leaves. She grew up with Helen, they're cousins, and she had no patience for her and even less for the men who believed she was divine. Penelope was glad when she ran off with Paris, and hoped it would be the last we'd hear of her.

She didn't understand that when Helen looked at a man he burned. It wasn't that she was so beautiful, no, not at all. Those stories are false, nothing but rumour and delusion. Her face was hard, all planes and edges, her forehead too high, her chin too long, her brow too heavy, but it didn't matter, because she was the great and glorious Helen, and when she looked at you you felt chosen, elevated above everyone else, and honestly believed that your life—so grey until now—was about to become golden.

Everyone knew the story. Leda had been raped by Zeus who had taken the form of a swan. Leda laid an egg from which Helen was hatched, and here she was, sixteen years later, the child of the greatest god himself, destined for Olympus. Some believed all this as fact, as undeniable as the bruise on your toe when you kick a stone and yet no matter what we thought of the tale, we all believed that to lie with her was to walk unscathed through fire. So we were eager, we were curious. When I caught my first glimpse of her I saw that for all her presence she had the air of a lost child. Her eyes pleaded *Help me* even as her posture threatened to bring down thunderbolts. You didn't doubt for a minute that she had nightmares, heard voices, burned candles for fear of the dark, wept with her head in her mother's lap. It was this combination of prowess and frailty that entranced so many of us. You wanted to lead her out to a green field and calm her as if she was a young mare.

Penelope hated all this. It made her spit. But with the kidnapping came a more pressing issue. "What are you going to tell Menelaus when he comes for your help? You know he'll come. He's probably on his way now."

I made a face that said she was talking nonsense, to which she responded by coming down off the ladder and gripping my beard with both hands. "Don't be naive. You know he is."

We'd all vowed allegiance to whomever Helen picked, a tactic to forestall civil war. Still, I argued. "It's been years. Besides, he has Agamemnon and all the others." I gestured vaguely toward the southeast, across the mainland toward Sparta, the centre of the world, the big smoke. "Why would he come all this way just for me?"

"Spare me the false modesty. You'd have to be as dead as dried fish before he'd go without you."

Still, I disagreed.

She blew air in disgust. Penelope was the least super-stitious of women, but like all Achaeans she was a fatalist, and she worried that we were entwined with Helen, caught the way ivy chokes a tree, and she was right, we should have run while we had the chance, for two days later Menelaus arrived. He found me in the barn sharpening a plough. He had old Nestor with him and that chancre Palamedes; the three of them stood backlit in the doorway.

"Brave Odysseus, son of Laertes."

"Menelaus. Friend. Brother." I smiled and opened my arms as if his presence brought joy to my heart instead of dread to my gut.

"May Zeus Earth-Shaker keep your roof posts strong," said Menelaus.

"Come in," I said, "honour my humble barn." I called for wine.

Though he was doing his best to be dignified, Menelaus looked haggard; after all, he was a gull, a cuckold, and now here he was calling on others to help him get his wife back. We waded through the niceties and then he got to the point and reminded me of the oath.

The oath had been my idea, and it had returned to snare me. At the time it had seemed shrewd given my growing doubts regarding the competition for Helen. You don't get a woman like her and simply go back to the farm and live a contented life, no, you get more, a lot more, too much: envy and bitterness, and men trying to steal her, exactly what Paris did, leaving Menelaus looking like a pig on a platter.

The point was this: if I backed out I'd pay. If ever I needed help none would come, and even if that time never came, Menelaus and his big brother Agamemnon would be sure to take revenge, arranging accidents, burning my farm, maybe stealing Penelope or Telemachus. My name would be dirt and their lives a torment. So we stood there, me, Nestor-the-bore, Menelaus-the-cuckold, and Palamedes-the-haemorrhoid. The horses swivelled their ears to listen, the cows swung their heads to watch; the cats, the goats, and even the pigeons in the rafters and the mice in the hay became attentive. The sunlight poured in silt-rich and radiant, so that the air looked filled with gold dust and all you had to do was scoop it up in your palm and pour it into your pouch to be a rich man.

Menelaus talked about Trojan gold and everything else we could win. "It's about honour," he said. "Paris betrayed me. Betrayed all of us. Broke truce. Nine days I entertained him. Nine days I gave him everything he wanted, girls, boys, wine. And yet when I go off to my grandfather's funeral, what does he do, that piece of shit, that goat's ass, but steal my wife! I gave him hospitality and he robbed me!"

Nestor and Palamedes had clearly heard this rant before. They shifted impatiently, and when Menelaus finally wound down Palamedes spoke up. "Ships and men, Odysseus. We want ships and men. Plus cattle, grain, and wine."

"Wine," I said, wondering what had become of my order for a jug.

Palamedes was shark-smiling. He enjoyed seeing me squirm. He had a narrow skull, a crow's nose, eyes close-set and small, a short damp black beard that made me think of pubic hair. He knew I was stalling. There was no doubt he was shrewd, and he had a soul like pit lime. He thought he'd been through my brain like a termite through wood and seen everything inside me. Well, balls to him, I thought. I raised my arms priest-wise and began to sing, not words but yelps, and I resumed my plough filing, the noise rasping my skull bone while I howled and yipped and my visitors stared. Their shocked eyes told me that I was onto a good ruse. I kept at it, scraping at that blade until Menelaus put his fists to his ears. Then I dropped the rasp and picked up a goat and harnessed her to the plough. I did the same with a lamb then I stood back and pissed on my feet. I gave them a good soaking, but saved enough to wash the dust from my road-weary guests, the least I could do as a good host. They leapt like cats. Menelaus stared, looking around to see if there were other madmen in the barn, as if maybe all Ithaka was possessed, an island of lunatics. He backed away toward the door. Nestor was right with him, the two of them thinking no way, we don't want this crazy bastard Odysseus along. But Palamedes wasn't going for it. There's always someone who just doesn't like you and wants to see you fall. Palamedes was that man.

I wasn't done yet, though. I churned up a good froth of spit so that I foamed at the mouth. I was about to start barking, but at that moment Telemachus ran in shouting about the strange ship in the bay. Palamedes picked him up and held him like a fond uncle ready to pop a fig into his mouth, and in one smooth motion drew his knife and put it to my son's throat and gave me a querying look.

"I'll prepare my ships," I said, flat-voiced and hard.

Palamedes smiled. A cool triumph for him, one he savoured like another man's wife, while for me a humiliation that's followed me right up to the present.

"Odysseus?" asked Menelaus, frowning, bewildered at the performance he'd just witnessed.

I muttered something about too much wine at lunch and then made a show of plunging my head into a water trough.

Menelaus became brisk and practical, telling me that the fleet gathered at Aulis in thirty days.

I nodded as if I'd have it no other way and at that moment, as if on cue, Old Niko limped in with the wine and we all drank to a swift victory. So it was off to Troy for the brave Odysseus.

*

When Menelaus and his cronies had departed and Telemachus was put to bed, Penelope and I walked up the hill through the tart scent of citrus in the cool of the evening. I told her everything that had happened in the barn. When I reached the part about Palamedes putting his knife to Telemachus's throat, she staggered and clutched my arm so tightly her nails drew blood. "His time will come," I said, putting on a bold show of confidence I didn't feel.

The cart track led up and over the ridge to where the wind blew hard from the sea. We sat down and watched the quarter moon through the shredded clouds. The dark sea gleamed silver where the moonlight hit. The scent of grass and mint sweetened the salt breeze. I put my arm around my wife—she smelled of lavender and fear and trembled with rage, not only at Palamedes but at Helen, because she'd hoped we'd finally got out from her shadow.

"Ten weeks and I'll be back," I said. "Shall I give Helen your love?"

Penelope looked at me with those green eyes of hers that begged me not to joke. I pressed her hand. They say the Scythians believe that the hand is the house of the soul, for everything we do is via the fingers, eating, making love, killing. An interesting notion, though if I were pressed to choose an organ I would opt for the tongue.

"I hate Palamedes."

"And he hates me," I said, though I couldn't say whether this meant anything. He'd grown even more arrogant and ambitious since I'd seen him nine years ago and he'd kept close to Menelaus and Agamemnon. I could understand Menelaus not seeing through him, after all, he'd let Paris walk off with his woman. But Agamemnon? "I expect I'll see young Ajax," I said, changing the subject.

She ignored this. "Telemachus will miss you," she whispered.

Reassuring myself as much as her, I said that he had a lot to divert him. We sat a long time thinking about him. We even managed to laugh a little at all of the questions he'd been asking of late. Where do the waves come from? Can I climb a ladder and pick clouds? And there were his ongoing efforts to tame spiders and befriend beetles. Toward a father one feels ultimate loyalty; to a son ultimate obligation. Not that we were alike in all things, not at all. He loved fishing while I never had the patience to stand there holding a stick and a string. He's small for his age, (something for which he can blame both his parents), but quick and as agile as an acrobat, with Penelope's green eyes and my bow legs. When Penelope went into labour I smeared the house in pitch against evil spirits and then afterwards hung the olive branch over the door. I held him when he was born and he looked at me as though he knew me, as if he already had opinions, as if he'd been listening the entire time he'd been in his mother's belly. He evaluated everything, the oil lamps, the braids of garlic, the bundles of sage and thyme dangling from the rafters. I suspect he knew the answer to the question of all questions, which is not where we go after death but where we are before birth, except by the time he could talk he'd forgotten.

"I'll be home by the solstice," I said. "We'll break the ice on the pond together." It was a small ritual of ours to step out at dawn as the pale sun rose and go in search of ice.

Argos had followed us and now began to whine.

"He knows," she said.

"Dogs always know." We regarded the pup, scarcely half a year old, awkward and lanky and still stepping on its ears. I placed my palm cap-like over his skull and asked him not to forget me. The dog watched me with large eyes rheumy with sap, as if it understood, and maybe it did. Dogs and even chickens always knew when a storm or earthquake was coming.

Penelope began to sob so I put my arm around her and pretended to be brave. When she'd recovered she looked at me with her chin set hard as a wedge, and in a resolved voice demanded I do something for her.

"Tell me."

"Kill Palamedes."

*

The next morning I went for advice to my father, Laertes, and found him talking to his cat, a fat orange tom missing an ear. He called this cat Fish. He thought this clever, because the cat was always prowling around ponds and streams and tidal pools, and was surprisingly quick with its paws for a beast who spent so much time asleep. My father and mother had gone into retirement in a house of planks and stone overlooking both the orchard and the bay. When I arrived he was peeling an apple as if unwinding a ball of string, cutting the peel as thin as possible to see how long he could make it. Such are the activities that occupy old age. When he saw me he nudged the cat with his toe.

"Didn't I tell you, Fish. Eh? He'll be up. He'll be calling and wanting advice." He laughed. "Too bad it's the one gift the young are so incapable of accepting. I believe this is called a paradox. *We are too soon old and too late smart / Age and wits pass each other in the dark.*"

"I'm twenty-nine. Not all that young, and maybe not utterly deaf to wisdom."

He made a face as if to say to the cat: well, well, listen to this. He continued peeling, or unwinding as it seemed, the apple. I knew enough not to push him, to let him talk when he felt ready in his roundabout way. Finally he started recalling his time with the Argonauts, and how he'd resented

Jason demanding he go along because I was only four and it meant a long separation. It still hurt to think of those seven years apart from me and my mother, he said, though he also admitted that nowadays it gave him hours of pleasure to remember all he'd seen and done, that a good store of memories was more valuable than gold to an old man. "I drank my cup to the dregs," he said. "As to whether I was wise to go along on another man's quest, well . . ." He shrugged. And with that he finished the apple, measuring out the peel along the entire length of his arm from his fingertips to his shoulder. "Not bad. Not bad." He dangled the peel before the cat, who batted it once with his paw and then yawned. Laertes, taking this for a judgment, shrugged and tossed the peel to a goat and began to eat the apple, seeming to forget I was even there.

I remember how when he at last returned he was a stranger, as awkward with me as I was with him. My mother welcomed him with all the warmth due a returning hero, but there was a distance, a formality. It took months before he seemed a natural part of our lives. He was a great man, an adventurer, one of the Argonauts, a comrade of Herakles. He returned with a reputation and an endless store of tales of far off places and famous events, yet there was a remoteness in his eyes. As if he had looked at things that a man shouldn't, things he couldn't forget even though he wanted to.

When he left I missed him, and when he returned I was disappointed at this much discussed man who was so much smaller than I'd recalled, as lean as a beggar, and worst of all had hair tufting from his ears. When he embraced me I saw those hairs up close. They were long and straggly and stank of ear wax. Old men had hairy ears. My father was not only a stranger but old.

Had I been ten years younger I might have regarded sailing off to Troy as an adventure; at twenty-nine I did not. At twenty-nine I was still strong, but I could also see, like a city coming into view through the dust and distance, that I was approaching a place where I'd only be weaker and slower, where one day my arm would shake as I drew my bow, and my sight would dim as if I lived in twilight. Besides, I'd been enjoying life on Ithaka. Few things are as satisfying as harvesting your own crops, making wine, and presiding over the birth of livestock. The goats entertained me, the hens soothed me, I admired the hunting skills of the barn cats, and even came to appreciate the dull dignity of cows. Most of all I feared leaving Penelope and Telemachus, the two creatures above all others who gave purpose to my existence. What were prizes and reputation without them? And yet to remain here under a cloud of scorn would only bring them humiliation.

Chapter Two

WHEN I WAKE I think for a blessed moment that I'm back in Ithaka and that the entire war is a bad dream sent down by some meddling god. Then I see the tent, my armour, my helmet with its boar tusks, and I groan and put my hands to my face. When I eventually sit up, a wave of dizziness nearly topples me back over. I brace myself with my hands and sit a long time staring at my legs. Are those scarred limbs mine? Is it possible that I'm thirty-nine years old? Looking at the backs of my hands I can well believe I'm turning into a pine tree, my skin coarse as bark, arteries exposed roots, knuckles gnarled knots.

Sleeping in the afternoon is a bad habit. Even with a cross-breeze, the heat leaves me muddled so that I inevitably wake feeling hungover instead of refreshed, and yet more and more I feel the need to withdraw each day, for a while at least, not to court the Muse or ponder Great Things —bugger all that—but to brood. My tent is stark. I've got my blades and my bow, and a cedar trunk that holds my clothes and letters, as well as a few clever little boxes with compartments within compartments that hide rings and

coins and the odd pearl, and of course I have the armour of
Achilles, the one notable prize I've collected. One of
Sinon's chores is to polish that armour so that it always
gleams. Otherwise I lead a dull existence. The tent pole is a
lance of ash; the floor an ox's hide. Gathering the strength
to move, I press my hands down on my thighs and, groaning
again, stand up, ride out another wave of dizziness, and step
outside into the waning afternoon.

As usual, most of the men are scattered off along the
beach looking under rocks and peering into the shallows
seeking something to eat. We spend less and less time on
strategy and training and more on scrounging, or simply lying
around. Entire days I've waded the tidal pools or lain on
rocks studying the antics of crabs. Other days, I walk the
shore where the land has buckled, reading the exposed strata
of rock and soil in all its variety, as if the very earth itself had
been formed in layers like the rings of a tree. Is it possible
that the earth is growing, adding a new layer each year, and
that by digging down and down you might read its rings and
learn its age? And does it follow that it will grow bigger and
bigger until it touches the sun?

Such ideas occur when I drink poppy water and end
up staring at my reflection in a pool. A disorienting experience to be thus multiplied, a me here, a me there, Odysseus
in the flesh and Odysseus in the water. That this phenome-
non is a trick of light does not lessen its disturbing nature. Of
course, poppy and idleness are unhealthy habits that breed
dark whims, such as what would occur if there were two
pools, or ten, all ranged around me so that I saw a dozen

Odysseuses, each acting independently, desiring to escape from their glassy imprisonment, calling for help in the voices of drowned men.

Those men who aren't foraging wander about farting and scratching and yawning, their clothes ragged with wear. The whores cuff their runts who whine for the teat while the dogs glide as silent as sharks. Hungry, everyone chews their fingernails. Soon the fires are built up, and as the sun begins to decline the shadows of our tents stretch long over the sand. The stench of the tanners is all through the camp, ox and horse hides and goatskins scraped and scalded then stretched to dry. We boil the bones for broth, the hooves for glue, and keep the sinews for bowstrings and cordage.

I totter down to the water, strip, and plunge into waves that rear like horses, white-maned with foam. Achaeans don't generally like to swim because they fear Poseidon and his harem of nymphs. The ocean is no doubt a strange thing, as vast perhaps as we can imagine, and full of even stranger creatures, many of which I've seen in the nets of fishermen. But I swim with my eyes open, for the salt water soothes them.

When I wade out of the sea, Dercynus pours a bucket of river water over me to rinse off the salt, oils me with orange flower, a gift from Agamemnon's private stock, and then kneads the muscles in my neck and shoulders, working thoroughly with his thumbs from the base of my skull on down. He has good hands, Dercynus, stronger than Sinon's. When he's done he presents me with a fresh tunic, white with blue trim, though worn so thin that it is almost as translucent as a dragonfly's wing. Not one of Dercynus's nobler chores, washing my clothes, but he never complains. Unlike the ironic Sinon, who'd go into a washerwoman's voice and make me laugh as she lamented her lot.

Dercynus has one blue eye and one brown; people don't know whether to assume him cursed or blessed. Either way, his vision is keen and he's always the first to spot the evening star. He's stockier than Sinon, square-shouldered and a stronger wrestler, (I'm still better but not for long), and as fast a runner as I was at his age. He lacks Sinon's wit and manner, but he's observant and he puts both of his eyes, the blue and the brown, to good use.

Sinon arrives with a platter of meat and a bowl of wine, play-acting like a tavern waiter, "Nuffing but the finest fer Ordysheus, wiv de complerments uv Argeememneeon." The horse meat is sinewy and the wine sour, but I'm grateful for usually it's boiled barley and seaweed. It's not uncommon for a man to cut an artery in a horse and suck a mouthful of blood. I've done it myself; a rich hot broth, though glutinous, and the taste lingers and gums up your teeth unless you rinse your mouth with lemon, or, given the scarcity of fruit, a mouthful of sea water. I always thank the horse after I've drunk its blood, it's only polite after all, and look into its eyes as I offer my appreciation, those dark orbs dim with ideas that never quite bloom. Sheep are a different beast altogether, their eyes as opaque as mud. Goats, however, are the most manlike of them all, the yellow crevices through which they spy on the world of men make me believe in satyrs. Dogs interbreed and share characteristics, why not man and goat?

"Come on, eat. Don't stand there staring." Sinon and Dercynus dig in. There's more than enough and I don't eat nearly as much as I once did. Besides, it's a pleasure to see them gorge. What beautiful young men: complexions clear, foreheads smooth, hair thick, their eyes free of veins. No need to pluck the hair from their ears. Sinon favours white tunics because he likes the contrast with his olive skin, whereas Dercynus opts for dark. Altogether an earthier fellow, Dercynus, a man of the soil, a farmer at heart, at ease with digging. He can cup soil in his hands and inhale its scent as if it is a bowl of hot stew while Sinon will worry about his nails.

"Look at them," says Dercynus, those strangely paired eyes of his round and wide, and his lips glum as he nods toward the shoreline.

We watch men scouring the beach, stepping carefully on the kelp-slick stones seeking mussels, eels, crabs, anything they can stomach. The way they bend to pry up rocks it looks as if they are sowing seeds to grow fish. Each time they straighten to ease their backs they take a moment to squint against the glare off the water—and doubtless lay down a curse on the heads of Menelaus and Helen—then bend once more to the task.

Dercynus says he hears their talk at night, that their patience is gone.

As sour as it is, I drink all my wine, suck at the meat skewer and then work my gums with the stick. How I miss hot bread and sweet onions. If I murdered Menelaus and Agamemnon, thus freeing the men to refit their ships and sail home, I'd be secretly loved, and yet at the same time publicly vilified, my name synonymous with treachery, a burden my son would bear long after I'm dead.

Dercynus draws in the dirt with his finger and observes that it will be hunger before homesickness that drives the men to desertion. He stares at his feet and frowns as if the tally of his toes is off.

"Home? I hardly remember home," says Sinon, knuckling away an invisible tear and performing the quavering voice of a maudlin waif causing both Dercynus and I to smile. "Where's me home? Where's me mum? Where's me dad? Where's me bum?"

Sinon and Dercynus-strange-eyes were press-ganged on the eve of the fleet's departure from Aulis. Servants for the kings. Agamemnon's orders. But they are my obligation as well, my wards, adopted sons, and I've taught them, though they have taught me a few lessons as well, such as patience. Ten years old when they were given to me. Children. Sinon still peed himself at night. When he or Dercynus wept it was to me they came running for solace.

I scrub my hands with sand and then contemplate the declining sun burning huge on the horizon. As it begins to set the clouds redden, and when the sun is gone the backlit sky glows like the wall of a kiln.

In the evenings there's little more to do but lie and complain, taunt each other, reminisce and listen to the old tales. Every one of us is a connoisseur of stories, recognizing a new emphasis here, a variation there—*in fact they were twins separated at birth; the father had been married before; the raven was in fact Zeus, she was the offspring of a god*—the tales handed down like figurines polished by each set of hands through which they pass.

When the tales are done there is always the fire to watch, each fuel creating a distinct flame: blue sparks erupting from salt-cured driftwood, the smooth burn and sharp heat yielded by bark so different from the rolling white smoke from damp fir branches, or sapwood that spits like fat. The flames sway like dancers, sometimes frenzied, sometimes slow, and yet always entrancing. No one among us loves fire more than Diomedes, who sees radiant cities in the quaking coals, empires erupting in burning twigs, titanic battles when sapwood screams; when a gust bends the flames flat it's a fleet of ships running downwind, pennants flying. He's the most handsome of all the captains, his face perfect in its symmetry, square forehead and jaw, straight nose, full lips, even teeth. Only the expression in his eyes betrays his incorrigible irreverence. He kills like a cat, a hunter born to the task, yet I suspect he'd just as soon juggle oranges in the market as gain glory on the battlefield. *Reputation, Odysseus, we're prisoners of reputation . . .* I often throw questions at him: *Diomedes, where does fire go when it's not burning?* Entering into the spirit of the farce, he'll say: *The same place as the wind. I see, and tell me, you clever duck you, why do men have nipples? Ah, that's obvious, because we're all women in the womb before Zeus picks out the ugly ones.*

We have musicians, of course. Or more accurately, men who strum the citharis, blow flutes, and sing, men who, by now, should be skilled yet still punish their instruments like peasants beating their mules. I just don't like Achaean music, something I keep to myself. I'd be wise to keep most of my thoughts to myself. I rarely speak to anyone of my Dreams, especially the ones that recur. There is one that comes down and whispers in my ear of a world without gods, a world that has no beginning or end, a world that was, is, and always will be, a world of ice and sky, rock and bone, a world without colour. In this Dream I walk the earth hearing nothing but wind. Afterwards, when I wake from this grim vision, I lay on my side as if struck down by a fist. And yet at other times I suspect that dreams are but the day's events flooding the banks of our waking hours into the fertile plains of night, an over-strung bow shooting an arrow beyond the horizon of day into the realm of sleep.

For years I've been asking everyone I meet if they've ever seen a god. Many insist they have, but it only takes a few careful questions to reveal that it was always foggy or they were drunk (ah, Dionysus, they say humorously, knowingly, winking at the god in the grape). Or they explain that it wasn't a god as such but a god in the form of an eagle or a snake. And what did this snake do that so distinguished it from others of its kind? Talk? Fly? Offer you a drink of wine? No, not really, you had to be there. The gods are beyond words. Indeed from what I can gather they most commonly manifest themselves as voices whispering in your ear. And I've heard a lot of those.

I don't doubt the gods, but I sometimes hate them. Often as a boy I sacrificed to Hermes to carry a message to my father the Argonaut asking him to return. Months I offered fruit, birds, coins, fine stones from the creek, and polished shells from the sea, the most valuable things I had, but he did not return. I gave up. I no longer had a father. And then years later a man appeared claiming to be Laertes. He looked more like a beggar than a king, and I thought that the gods were laughing at me. That's when I began to hate the gods.

*

I hate Menelaus and Agamemnon as well. They're right about one thing though: the time has come, in fact it's long passed. The Trojans lost Hector and we lost Achilles. Their best and ours. And yet we're no closer to resolving this stalemate. I head off up the shore to walk and think, because my brain works better when my body is occupied. I don't get far, however, before a voice calls: "Odysseus." It's Agamemnon.

"A busy world," he says as I join him. The front legs of his chair are propped on a log and the headrest is high enough that he can view the stars without straining his neck. We gaze in silence. When a shooting star marks the sky like a streak of chalk, Agamemnon grunts. "Messengers." He sounds troubled, assuming that of course the message is about him, the big man, the great king, that he's been waiting for this dispatch from the gods in council concerning our grubby bit of business down here on our briny beach. Then his right hand rises and brushes it aside as though tired of it all, and I sense that his mood is not due to Troy and Priam and the war, but something more personal: his wife. We've all heard the rumours about her and Aegisthus. No one dares joke, because we all fear the same may be happening behind our own backs.

"We'll be home soon," I reassure him, though I won't deny a small satisfaction at seeing him troubled like this, even if it means some of his frustration might be vented upon me.

"And what will I find?"

"Your people."

He snorts.

How different we are in the night. The light gone, the moon up, the lurkings of our minds rise like glowfish to feed.

"They hate me. The men hate me. You hate me."

I swallow this bone without flinching. "Love, hate. These things come and go. Hot winds and cold. Balance," I say, "the true kernel of the matter. All things find their equilibrium. After ten years we're overdue for a turn in our fortunes."

He asks me if I believe this and I lie and say yes.

"There." Another star chalks the dark. "A lot of talk tonight."

The origins of fire, the secrets of the stars, these are eminently intriguing topics—Hermes dashing about with messages—but I don't believe that every light in the sky, every glow in the sea, every snake that crosses your path is a mystery or a portent. Sometimes things are only things, a rock a rock, a skull a bit of bone. And who knows, the gods but idle ghosts.

"The men are talking," Agamemnon says.

"They always talk."

"They blame me for Achilles," he goes on, ignoring me, and yet at the same time hoping I'll prove him wrong. I can almost hear his thoughts: *Come, Odysseus, arrange some words, convince me of how popular I am.* "They think that without him we'll be defeated. That we're doomed. And it's my fault."

I make noises to the contrary, but it's true, the men do blame Agamemnon, and for good reason. He should have left Briseis to Achilles, he should have known how Achilles would react, how anyone would react. But for all Agamemnon's experience, for all his kingly wisdom, he's a clod. He was always threatened by Achilles who was younger, stronger, better looking, and had the ears of the gods. He feared him and was jealous of him, so he got rid of him. The tautest bow is also the most easily broken.

"I should cut their tongues out."

Is this for my benefit? Does he suspect me of talking, of spreading discontent? "Swift victory is the surest route to respect."

"And you know how to achieve this?" The childlike hopefulness in his tone is almost endearing.

"I'll find a way." I speak with more confidence than I feel. But Agamemnon is desperate for reassurance. He doesn't want to hear how tricky it will be, the long odds, the high risks. I stand then say goodbye and leave him to his stars and his gloom and the doubt gnawing like rats at his heart.

What a relief to walk. The camp stretches out along the coast so that we've cut off Troy's access to the sea, though they still have a corridor to the Scamander. For years our camp has been a city unto itself, if rather long and thin, between water on one side and dirt on the other, until recently lacking nothing, meat, wine, women, boys, acrobats. But the supply convoys arrive less frequently now, the usual pimps and purveyors who dog armies have drifted off because we no longer have the money to pay. The war has dragged on and bankrupted us all, so that we're raiding up and down the coast, which doesn't exactly endear us to the locals. We live in tents, cook over driftwood fires, shit in the sea, and more and more resort to eating rats and kelp. By Agamemnon's order, no permanent structures are built, lest we grow complacent and lose our fighting spirit. Lose it? Ha. It's long gone. After so many years it's tough to maintain the belief that victory's near and that we'll soon be home. Men who arrived young have withered and died, for this sort of warfare defeats you the way rot kills trees, slowly, from within, weakening the core, turning the spirit to dust. Desertions have become commonplace, men so crazed that they wade into the sea and simply start swimming west. We don't execute them; we can't afford to, and I admit that I've often imagined trying the same thing. Those are the same nights I think about my son, and about something else, which is that the only man I hate more than Menelaus, Agamemnon or Palamedes is myself for not having found an honourable way of staying home.

A half moon is pressed like a bent coin into the sky, throwing a path of light across the ocean. My left kneecap aches, thanks to a kick from a Trojan who had my bronze-tipped spear in his throat. He caught me a sharp one on the kneecap—more of a spasm of the leg than a well-aimed blow—but it nearly crippled me all the same. Another injury to add to the list: the numb hands, the locked back, the torn ear, the broken toes, and sprained fingers. Some scars I'm proud of, the tusk-gash on my thigh received while boar hunting with my grandfather was my first, and it remains the one of which I am the most fond. More and more I feel like a battered old tomcat. More and more I hate both the Achaeans and the Trojans and all their gods. Enough. The company of these men has grown stale. The prostitutes who service us are fouler of mouth, grosser of figure, and tougher of hide than the men, the sex closer to relieving your bladder than rapture, much less intimacy. As for their bawling spawn of runts, they generally drown them, and if not they're fated to a life of mischief, cowering about the camp like dogs, slimy-nosed and filthy-fingered, their vocabularies even more appalling than that of their mothers.

The wise and fatherly Agamemnon—our leader, our Zeus, our Man among Men—growing concerned for our well-being has ordered us to undertake a daily regimen of callisthenics. (Masculinity being an achievement not a fact of birth.) We run and wrestle and box, and take pride—so the theory goes—in the realm of maleness; and lest our brains rot, he encourages elevated debate to keep body and mind in balance, like the spread wings of an owl. Yet how lonely the owl seems. I miss the murmur of women and the genial chaos of children who know awe at a world always new. The army bastards are nothing but a whining subspecies who rarely live three years before the bloody flux carries them off. It would be wiser to put the whores and their whelps onto a barge and ship them off, but not even Agamemnon is willing to risk depriving the noble Achaeans of such solace.

And so I take long walks. Off to my left our ships rot at anchor, overdue to be beached and have their beards scraped. For all Agamemnon's vigilance, our boats are turning to kindling. I've warned him but he worries that to set men to repairing the ships will only give them the means of escape. He's even gone so far as to order that no men go aboard in case their thoughts stray. Nonetheless, I sometimes exercise privilege and go onto mine and sleep in my old berth. Telemachus loved the ship, the eyes on the blue hull convincing him that it was not merely a clever construction of wood and rope, but a creature as alive as a dolphin, and like a dolphin breathing the air but inseparable from the sea. And who knows, maybe there's some truth to this. A ship seems a living creature breathing the wind on the glittering water. Penelope loved the ship too, though I suspect with a certain wariness, fearing that it must inevitably take me away. Against this possibility, she carved all our names on the bulkhead by my bunk, Penelope, Telemachus, Odysseus.

Beyond the sand hills and beach pines stands Troy, the new Babylon, the new Nineveh. Well, we know what happened to them. Sand and dust, home to nothing but the rat and the vulture. I plod on, footsteps filling with water, waves thumping the sand, my mouth heavy with the taste of sour wine and seared horse, food that sits like mud in my gut.

Crabs put up their claws and side-scuttle into their holes. I like crabs, they've got personality. Telemachus used to lure them with a bit of meat on a stick. He had such patience for a four-year-old, such focus. Sooner or later the crabs would edge back up and Telemachus would snag them and look at me with pride.

Bait—that's the key. Every creature can be lured. What will lure the Trojans from their hole? What do they want, besides us to go away? I try going at the problem on the oblique, for that's the best means of spotting solutions, from out of the corner of your eye. Look too directly and the answer vanishes like a mouse. Chewing my nails, I ponder. I begin thinking about my fingernails, about bird talons and dog claws, how it is that we all have them, man and beast, lizard and bird, and I wonder if there is anything to conclude in this, some grand truth other than that we all need to scratch. Penelope painted hers blue. Oh, for the delicious feel of them raking my back once again. A good long scratch is as good as sex, but the two together—ecstasy. What do the Trojans prize? Fish are lured by worms. Horses by apples. A buzzard by carrion. Achaeans love their boats. The Trojans? In their hearts they're people of the plains, with their backs to the sea and their faces to the steppe, toward Cappodoccia, Persia, India, and therefore it's obvious that they prize nothing above the horse.

A horse.

O Muse, subtle as the wind-borne scent of thyme . . .
But clearly not just any horse would do. No. Perhaps many
horses, a herd of Scythian mares, or else one single splendid
specimen, a giant stallion of pure silver. Where would we get
a silver horse? Pool our precious metals and cast one? I can
hear the remarks already: give sly Odysseus our silver, our
gold? Ha.

Seawater fills my footprints and each one holds a half
moon. A dead-fish wind idles along the shore and the mus-
cling waves slide over the sand. I look again at the towers of
Troy. Yes, a people who liked things big, high walls, high
towers, massive gates. To be honest, a little on the crude
side, peasants at heart, like the northern barbarians. But
there's mettle to them, they're dogged and they have more
pride than a Pharaoh, but a bit blinkered and easily dazzled.
So it'll have to be a big horse, the biggest they've ever seen,
one they'll lust for, one so huge they'll gladly creak open
those spiked gates and haul it inside because a horse so enormous can only be a Sign, and let's face it all men are fools for
Signs, all of us believe an eclipse or a snake or a summer hailstorm means that the gods are near, that divine forces are at
work, that the end can be seen at the beginning. Even I took
heart when a heron appeared the night Diomedes and I cut
up the Thracians.

I'm walking faster now, brain wheels grinding. The
coast juts and scallops with points and bays, the wind-
stunted cedars are good only for firewood or crutches, not
god-like wooden horses. Big jobs demand oak, straight and
tall, and the best stands are on Mount Ida. We can fell the

trees and float them down the Scamander and start work, though that will take too much time and too much labour. It will mean half a year or more.

Soon I smell creek mud and then mosquitoes hit me like a fistful of hot sand. I spin away and spot our ships in the moonlight. We've lost so many men that we don't have crew enough to sail half of them home. We'll have to burn them, or—and here blessed Muse graces me again—our carpenters can unbind the planks of one and use them to build a horse, a horse the like of which no one has ever seen before, a horse not even Herakles could ride, a horse with a surprise in its belly . . . I begin to run, indifferent to my bad knee, waving my arms mad-fool-wise about my head to shoo the bugs. Hearing my laughter the dogs howl with rage for they sense that the tide of war is about to turn.

Chapter Three

I HAD, OF COURSE, anticipated debate. With Achaeans there's always debate. We thrive on it. But Ajax is even more blunt than usual.

"This is a shit plan," he says, regarding me as if I'm nothing but a wandering pedlar, a vagrant of the roads trying to beguile them with stale tricks. He finishes sucking a fish spine then makes a performance of tossing it into the fire. Belching richly, he draws his baby finger across his lips (for he's not without delicacy, our Ajax).

I could have presented an army of ten thousand strong soldiers and Ajax would find something to complain about. *Too short, too slow, no discipline. A hindrance. More trouble than they're worth . . .* Bundles of cedar fronds smoulder against the mosquitoes. A wave crashes on the beach. Everyone awaits my reaction. I smile. I smile and incline my head as if honoured by the depth and subtlety of his analysis. "O wise one, how reassuring that I can always rely upon a considered response from you."

He's ready for this, and looks at me as if his glare

alone could crush my skull. Judging by the hate in his expression I almost believe it. He spits.

And yet what a charming boy Ajax had been when we first met. A young prince with royal manners. Though he was in Sparta to compete he was ingenuous and innocent and wished the other competitors well. He was a student of bees and spent entire afternoons in the clover with his chin on his fists studying those marvellous insects, making sketches, dissecting the small dry corpses and holding them to the sunlight, convinced that any creature that ate flowers and vomited honey had a god in it. He's lost that wonder and become coarse. Worse, he's grown rigid and blinkered, and what little sense of humour he once had has died.

"A shit plan," he repeats. "The Trojans aren't idiots. They'll laugh at this toy horse of yours."

The flames reflect in the shocked eyes of everyone around the fire. I glance toward Agamemnon, the one opinion that matters, but he merely watches, waiting for the others to have their say. For all that he needs my help he's not above taking some small pleasure in seeing me squirm. Certainly Palamedes does, but even he appears surprised at the vehemence with which Ajax dismisses me.

It is young Echion who speaks out, however. Echion the Eager, Echion the Impatient, incapable of sitting still. He can scarcely contain himself. "I like it. It's good. Let's build it!" He looks around eager for others to agree.

"Shut up," says Ajax, dismissing him. Ajax has many reasons for hating me. He thinks I've betrayed him for no longer playing the fond uncle, the older brother, the way I did when we first met so many years ago. He's also convinced I think he's a blockhead, that I've decided he has cheese for a brain. And then there's the little business of my defeating him in the games for Achilles's armour, a defeat he remains suspicious about, (a suspicion fuelled by Palamedes). How could runt Odysseus—older, slower, smaller —throw the mighty Ajax? How? It wasn't all that complex, there was no drug or god involved, no Egyptian curse or Phoenician sorcery. I kept low and caught him behind the knees and used his own weight against him. Plus I did something else, something that always succeeds, at least the first time around: I praised him. Yes, praised him. The day before the match, I paid him a visit and grew nostalgic about the old days, when we first got to know each other. I spoke the truth, telling him how he, fourteen-year-old Ajax, scarcely more than a boy, had struck fear into every man competing for Helen in Sparta. I talked for some time, pouring on the honey. He was wary at first, but no man can withstand such a siege of praise, in time it will wear him down the way wind erodes stone. After such a paean how could Ajax fight me, for we never go hard against friends, we always hold back. The real challenge was for me to fight as if I hated him. It was that or be defeated, or, worse, sit out the games altogether. Then what? Have them laughing at old Odysseus Has-Been-Once-Was?

The armour of Achilles is in my tent, wrapped in a blanket so that its fire-bright gleam doesn't torment Ajax. Only when he is away from camp do I take it out and admire it: bronze chest and back plates modelled to fit Achilles's torso, a bronze helmet topped with boar tusks and a crest of horsehair, a bronze-faced shield and bronze greaves for his shins. It's too large for me and too small for Ajax.

And now he and I are fighting again. "Ajax, if Achilles had come up with the idea you'd applaud it, wouldn't you? Be honest now."

"Honest? I'm always honest," says blue-eyed Ajax. "Ask anyone. It's my weakness. Yet you. This is just another one of your schemes, the only thing you contribute." He shakes his head implying that, unlike him, I drag behind me a long chain of inane ploys and clumsy deceits, such as my idea of digging a tunnel under the walls of Troy, or of using long poles for vaulting over them. Are these any worse than offering prayers and incense to gods no one's ever seen? I've also got a long history of fairly won victories. Why are these so easily forgotten? And why is it forgotten that Achilles tried avoiding Troy by dressing as a woman? Ajax doesn't like being reminded that his hero tried escaping this whole business just as I had done. Nor does Ajax like it that I'm the one who exposed Achilles's ruse.

"A wooden horse," says Ajax. "The Trojans will set fire to it, or . . ." He struggles for words. "Pry the planks apart and stab everyone inside like crabs in a bucket." He shrugs. He turns his hands palm upward and looks to Agamemnon, Menelaus, Palamedes, old Nestor, all of whom sit like a gallery of judges. "We know Odysseus could charm the fangs out of an adder. I'm not gifted with such a slithery tongue. But I've got eyes. I see what's what. Ever since Odysseus broke into the Trojan temple and stole the Palladium our luck has gone sour. It was supposed to gain us favour. I never understood how. But who listens to me? We're being punished. This is plain. And now he comes up with this."

The response is silence, and like all silences it's loud with brooding and doubt. The men seated around the fire draw down into themselves and stare into the flames, thinking of what they could be doing, what they *should* be doing, instead of being stuck here, far from their families and farms, growing old on this crumbling coast with an ever-diminishing prospect of going home. You only have to look to see we've had it. The firelight is both kind and cruel, hiding some scars and highlighting others. Armour keeps us alive, but can't prevent the mangled fingers, the lost ears, the crushed toes. Ajax is the only one who has all his teeth, miraculously because, to his undeniable credit, he marches foremost into every battle. His knees and arms have taken the worst, striped with slash wounds and puckered with stab marks. Agamemnon, along with his blunted nose, has lost the hearing in his right ear and has a back as rigid as a plank. Menelaus limps and has only half strength in his left hand. Old Nestor is blind in his left eye. Sinon's right collarbone was so badly broken he can scarcely heft a sword. Diomedes took one of Paris's arrows in the foot and limped for a year. Not even Palamedes has escaped injury—and no man protects himself more cleverly—he nearly bled dry from a gash across the side of the neck. None of us stands, sits, or reaches for a cup of water without a groan. Of the dead, few went quickly, lingering for days as their blood seeped through the tightest bandages. It's easy enough to avoid looking at a man as he drains away like a badly caulked barrel, but not so easy to avoid overhearing his agony. Every one of us reflected upon what Achilles said when Agamemnon took Briseis: *Fate is the same for the man who holds back and the man who fights his best.* Better a long and quiet life than one brief if glorious.

But Ajax has a point about the horse. It's a risk. A bold move, maybe a foolish one.

Uneasy with silence, Ajax starts in on me again: "The gods hate us because Odysseus denies they even exist!"

"Of course they exist," I say, quietly, sincerely (and I even believe it, for I'm not immune to my own words). "My own grandfather, Autolycus, was sired by no less than Hermes. That Hermes is sacred not only to messengers but to thieves and liars as well makes him no less a god," I add wryly, knowing perfectly well what everyone is thinking. Ajax tries to interrupt, but I raise my hand calling for patience, a moment to defend myself against such an egregious claim. "A world without the gods is a terrifying prospect . . . Of course, a world with the gods is—we must admit—also terrifying. The gods are such splendid creatures. Passionate. Fickle. Mysterious. A burning city is but a candle compared to the glory of Zeus. The beauty of Aphrodite finer than any sunrise. Hermes faster than any arrow. But perhaps this is not the point. The point is that everything exists. The air exists even though we can't see it. It pushes our ships, stirs trees, lifts the dust. We inhale it into our chests, exhale it from our nostrils, fart it from our arses. Light and dark exist. Songs stir our hearts and spur us on to victory. And yet what are songs but words, and what are words but air? And what about lies? Some lies contain truths and some truths the dark pearl of falsehood. Where is the man who has not acted honourably upon his sincere belief in a lie? Conversely, who has denied one truth in pursuit of a higher one? Where is the truth that is not a truth to one and a lie to another? Take, for instance, water—"

Ajax puts his fists to his ears. "Stop!"

The others hide their smiles.

It is Calchas, our soothsayer, who finally puts in his oar. "Spare us." He gazes around in his best effort at seeming profound. "Zeus does not tolerate disrespect." His tone made clear his meaning: I was close to blasphemy. A lesser man would have his tongue cut out.

"So now you speak for Zeus," I observe. "Tell us, what did he say the last time you two got together for a bowl of wine and a stick of meat?"

Calchas spits into the fire and grimaces as if I'm a bad taste. Sitting taller, he raises his chin as if to address higher things. "Ajax is right," he says. "Our luck has been bad. There must be a reason. For every result there is a cause. It is the thread that holds things. The fabric of the world."

"Suddenly our Calchas is a tailor." There are chuckles. Calchas grimaces in the direction of my voice. He's an ugly old man whose face looks like it's been carved from an onion. "Perhaps," I suggest, "there are many causes and effects. After all, no reasonable man will deny the variety of the world. Causes evolve into effects and effects in turn become causes. Both branch like rivers. And it only stands to reason that some causes are both more influential and indeed preferable than others."

Calchas makes a great show of yawning. It's said (by him) that as a boy a serpent licked his ears giving him the gift of prophesy. Snakes are undoubtedly among the most intriguing of creatures, but why they should have prophetic powers and be inclined to bestow them upon mortals, I'm sure I don't know. Nor can I understand the allure of putting my tongue in Calchas's ear. But to his credit, Calchas has done fairly well for himself by seeing portents in every thing and everywhere. He watches the battles from well back, and will never be seen scrubbing his own laundry. Reading signs is his way of making himself invaluable. When we were becalmed off Aulis he decided that the winds refused to carry us because Artemis was angry, and therefore Agamemnon's virgin daughter, Iphigeneia, must be sacrificed. Artemis? What did the goddess of the hunt have to do with wind? Calchas knew. Oh yes, he had it all sorted out. It was really quite simple: Artemis was angry with Agamemnon for having shot a stag in her sacred grove. To ask the location of this supposed grove was to be the meanest of hairsplitters. So Calchas said and so Agamemnon believed. He therefore called for his own daughter under the ruse that she was to marry Achilles. She arrived in a bronze-plated chariot pulled by two white stallions, with half the royal house as escort. The girl was ecstatic. Her eyes were glistening, her cheeks flushed, her breath sweet with mint, a nice looking young lady, firm of breast and round of hip, wearing a silk robe dyed in Tyrian purple. I suspect that even Achilles was tempted.

Whispering sweet words, Agamemnon put his arm around her shoulders and guided her into a grotto wreathed in olive branches where he cut her throat. Bled her over a stone. The rumour that the girl was not really his daughter, but Helen's via Theseus, hardly seemed an adequate excuse for such heartless, if strategic, butchery. And all this because of old Couch Ass.

Alright, the wind did begin to blow, but winds, like words, are variable things, as fickle as men, but try telling that to sailors suddenly blessed with a favourable breeze. How Calchas's spine straightened when that breeze quickened the air. His face dropped ten years. The captains applauded his powers and the oarsmen feared to look into his eyes. Who needs a strong arm when you have the ear of the gods? And perhaps Calchas does indeed see what he says? I don't need to be told that there are mysteries beyond reason. Why is a snake not poisoned by its own venom? How do frogs and crabs breathe equally well in either water or air? Why does Dionysus inhabit the grape but not the walnut?

The hunchbacked Calchas stands now with the help of his catamite, Telkinos, an intriguer if ever there was one. Calchas is forever gliding about with his right hand perched like a bird upon the boy's shoulder while Telkinos is forever whispering in Calchas's hairy old ear, as if he liked the smell of earwax. Now Calchas adjusts his leopard skin across his sloping shoulders (as if he's ever killed anything larger than a mouse or a mosquito!) and passes his hand over the fire as if to call up Hephaestus himself. "Athena is angry," he announces. "Angry at Odysseus."

I cross my arms and wait. My fault. Always is, always has been, always will be.

"Maybe she's angry at you," suggests Diomedes poking the coals. "It was *your* idea to take the Palladium. *You* read the signs. Odysseus and I merely did what you can't."

When the quiet man speaks he has an attentive audience. The others look to Calchas who responds dry-voiced and trembling. "Athena has long been our ally."

"No, *Odysseus* has long been Athena's favourite," says Diomedes.

As if cornered by dogs, Calchas becomes shrill-voiced and dire. "She carved the Palladium in honour of her sister. She demands compensation! Something valuable! A sacrifice! Either that or we'll stay here until we grow too tired to fight. Then the Trojans will drive us into the sea."

The company looks to me now, eager for my response. I leisurely toss a handful of hemp seeds onto the coals, and when they begin to smoke I inhale, once, twice, a third time. Diomedes leans in and does the same, bending the smoke into his lungs. My shoulders relax and I smile. Still, I say nothing. It never hurts to let the audience wait. True enough, the theft of the Palladium hadn't proved the success we'd all hoped, the Trojan spirit hadn't crumbled as soon as the statue was gone. I could have declined to take up the challenge in the first place, leaving it for Palamedes, but I wasn't about to give him such an opportunity. Besides, I'd regarded taking the statue as more of a rescue than a kidnapping, just like Paris snatching Helen. He did her a favour, or so he no doubt convinced himself (and I couldn't completely disagree, given Helen's alternatives in the lean and sinewy world of Sparta). So, a liberation. I liked the parallel. It had balance. It had symmetry. And I'm sure Athena thinks the same, if such a marvellous creature exists, and I rather hope she does, for how poor the world would be without her inspiration. If she hadn't wanted the image of her half-sister to leave Troy she'd have prevented it, wouldn't she?

It happened the previous year. Diomedes and I disguised ourselves. We raked our faces with thistles and clumped our hair with mud, and then we circled wide around the city, far out into the fields, waited until evening, and then staggered in calling for alms. We got ourselves a few coins, but mostly flung stones and some well-aimed kicks, but we got in. I was all set to head straight up to the temple but Diomedes took it into his head to step into a taverna and sample some Trojan beer. I tried to argue but it wasn't up for discussion. Diomedes is adamant about his whims. He lives for them, or they through him. He simply nudged me with his elbow and, affecting a grand manner, arms swinging, grin wide, strode across a plaza toward a crowd seated at benches flanking an open door. Above it hung a carved board depicting grapes and barley. Diomedes offered a jaunty wave to the good citizens. They didn't deign to notice two bums in need of a bath. Soon we were seated on a bench against a wall with a jug of beer. It was a tad bland for my taste, but Diomedes was having a fine time. He set his elbows on the plank table and, sleepy-eyed, as if he came here every evening to quench his thirst after a hard day, gazed around. The Trojans are on average taller and darker than Achaeans. They're emphatic and blunt. Even their simplest gestures, tossing down a coin, batting a fly, dismissing an irrelevant remark, are delivered with the assurance that comes from living in a great city. It's as if they think that simply by being in Troy their lives take place on a higher plane, that even grunting over their morning constipation is a more elevated activity.

"I miss city life," concluded Diomedes. "I think I could get on all right here." He raised his beaker to the barman for a refill and a serving boy limped over with a fresh jug and slopped our cups to the brim. Diomedes drank half in one go and then leaned close to my ear. "What do you think we just change sides?"

I smiled and picked a gnat from my mug. "It'd almost be worth it to see Agamemnon's face when he found out."

Diomedes clapped his thigh and let out his high howl of a laugh.

The taverna's stone walls were hung with tapestries depicting cows and lightning.

A one-armed man carrying a basket of eggs entered. In a well-rehearsed speech he announced that for a price he could stack nine eggs one atop the other. "And what do we get if you fail?" someone asked. "You get the eggs," he said, as if the answer should be obvious. He had the lean and watchful look of a man ever alert for an opportunity. I suspected he'd stolen the very eggs with which he was staging his trick. He got right down to work and began stacking the eggs. Soon a crowd had gathered. Diomedes joined them. I stood on a bench and watched from farther back. Two eggs, three, stacked end to end. The one-armed man gestured everyone away, no bumping the table, no hard breathing. Four, five, six eggs, each set just so, like brickwork. At the seventh egg someone grew suspicious and demanded to have a look at the others. The one-armed man held the three remaining eggs in his palm for all to inspect. "Fresh from the hen's arse." When the ninth egg was set on top everyone there, maybe fifty men, stared open-mouthed, as if Helen herself stood naked before them. The only sound was their breath through their beards. It was now dusk, and in the half-light of the oil lamps the men looked like troglodytes before the miracle of flame. Diomedes was the first to pay up. He tossed a coin that clattered on the table. Others followed, the coins ringing on the stone floor and wood benches. The one-armed man caught some in the air and pounced on the others like a cat on a rat. When he had every coin he briskly piled his eggs back in the basket. Someone shouted that they were hungry and wanted an egg but he was gone.

We finished out beers then followed the dirt street as it wound upward. Soon it was paved in neatly cut flags and flanked by fine villas. Feeling the beer, Diomedes enjoyed a leisurely piss against a wall. We reached the temple that sits high above the rabble with a view over the walls to the sea. "Not bad," said Diomedes, and I knew he was referring to the eggs. "The trick is salt. Did you notice how he put his hand into his pocket before placing each egg? The salt works like cement."

We hid beneath a fig tree and watched the stars.

"Salt?"

Diomedes nodded.

We listened to the sounds of Troy, harp and flute, a jug shattering, shrieks, barking. There was the syrupy scent of night blooming flowers.

When the moon had set we emerged. The Palladium is a wood statue of Pallas about my height, just over three cubits. In her right hand she grips a spear and in her left a distaff and spindle. Even in the dark it's impossible to miss her because she glows like a churned sea in the night. We approached with our eyes down whispering our apologies. Fresh roses were heaped around her. Wrapping her in a goatskin, we headed back down to the eastern gate and departed with the farm labour. We were far out in the fields when the cry arose and the trumpets sounded.

*

"Calchas is not altogether wrong," I say now, paying out some line. "The Trojans believe that without the Palladium they're vulnerable. So, yes, by all means, a sacrifice."

"What kind of sacrifice?" demands Agamemnon, dark-browed and suspicious, for we've nearly sacrificed ourselves dry and are down to offering up guts and hooves.

The highest sacrifice means a man and nothing less. This fact hung unspoken even as it was loud in everyone's mind.

I let Calchas have first say, but our seer, our diviner, our man intimate with the owl's mind and the eagle's heart, this man who had once condemned a young girl to the knife, suddenly becomes reticent. His mouth drops open as if to speak then claps shut, while his eyes withdraw deeper into their caves, wary of condemning someone to the slaughter stone. "I need more time," he croaks.

"You've had ten years," Agamemnon reminds him.

Calchas says nothing. Nor does anyone else. The spider of silence spins its web, for of course the question is: which man? A Trojan prisoner? Too cheap, too easy. It will have to be an Achaean, one of us. Nobody dares move much less name a name. I let the silence build. Every man there contrives to avoid the eyes of their neighbour. Who would be so selfless as to volunteer themselves? Who would be so cruel as to suggest a name?

I speak up cheerfully, as if the answer is simple. "You all know and love young Sinon." I extend my arm inviting him to step from out of the dark into the firelight. The expressions on the faces! The eyes of every man roll in terror at the fate to which I'm condemning the boy. Agamemnon watches and waits; Calchas is suspicious; Palamedes smiles his thin-lipped smirk, eager to learn what I'm up to. Sinon takes a demure pose, hands behind his back, and awaits my instructions. He's nineteen, slim, full-lipped, with long black hair and of course that smooth clean complexion of youth and the illusion of purity that comes with wearing white. What better sacrifice than a beautiful young man so excellent in every way? The horror on most every face is exquisite.

"The horse is only part of the scheme," I say, implying that only a fool and a simpleton—such as Ajax—could have imagined that it ended there, and that if they'd only have been patient I'd have already explained the rest. "We set the mood by building up the fires and putting on a show of some grand rite. Much song and lamentation. A tragic time for the noble Achaeans. The Trojans will see that something's up. They'll be curious. They'll go into council. Then Sinon slips away, into their territory, and lets himself be caught by their scouts. He begs their mercy. Pleads. A lot of boo hoo. Says he's fled because we intended to sacrifice him to Poseidon for a calm sea so that we—weary of this futile war against such an indomitable foe—can finally set sail for home."

Sinon now launches himself into a preview of his performance. He bends himself in his Protean way into old King Priam, dodders and dribbles and plays it up, earning a few smiles, even doing the accent, the way they swallow the ends of their words.

Priam: "Who are you, boy? Name your father. What do you mean by sneaking-thieving about our fair walls?"

Sinon: "King of kings, Lord of the Zeus-blessed Trojans, the foul Odysseus means to sacrifice me to Poseidon for a fair wind. Nothing less than human blood will do."

Priam: "Odysseus! A sister fucker if ever there was one."

Sinon: "To be sure, my lord, to be sure. A bum-sniffer of the lowest order."

Priam: "Give up a man for a wind? Barbarous. Come, Sinon. Forget the Achaeans. No enemy of theirs is an enemy of Troy. But tell us in plain words: what is the meaning of this wooden horse?"

Sinon: "Athena demanded reparation for the crime committed by the underhanded Odysseus. It was the only way she'd let the Achaeans depart alive. She hates them, and they knew they were beaten. They lamented around their fires each night."

Priam: "And how did Athena make her request known?"

Sinon: "Through Calchas."

Praim: "Ah, wisest of the Achaeans."

Sinon: "The owl of Minerva takes flight from his shoulders, sir. Make the horse yours. Sacrifice to it. Athena will love you."

Priam: "I have grown to suspect that the gods love no one but themselves. Perhaps we'll sacrifice you. What would you say to that?"

Sinon: "If Priam wills it, then I accept."

Sinon kneels and offers his neck to the old king's sword. Then, after a long and dramatic silence during which only the fire talks, he withdraws to a chorus of enthusiastic murmurs.

But his performance doesn't move Ajax. No, it's little more than chaff tossed at a rock wall. He doesn't like Sinon, regarding him as all too clever and mercurial. For Ajax, a man is only a man if he stands firm in the face of the enemy, keeps his mouth shut and lands his blows. He merely crosses his arms over his chest and looks away.

Nor is Palamedes impressed. "Surely, Odysseus, you don't think this *serving* boy will convince Lord Priam—ruler of the greatest city in the world—to abandon his senses and open gates he's defended with his own sons for ten years?" He gazes at me apologetically, as if sad at having to be the one to speak so hard a truth. The crow-black gleam in his eyes betrays his joy in pointing out such a glaring flaw, for he can't bear the idea that I win fame by getting us into Troy. Better we stay here, stuck, than see Odysseus celebrated.

"Palamedes," I say, putting on the humble voice. "I'm laid bare. Yes, I'm desperate. I'll explain why. Menelaus and Agamemnon—kings, leaders, warriors before whom we all kneel—came to me requesting aid. What an honour! To be so regarded is in itself prize enough. I've rendered small service before, night actions, furtive exploits, and ever with the stalwart Diomedes to steady me." Standing up, I reach out to include all the listeners beyond the firelight and, tucking my chin to give my voice bass, clench both my fists to my chest. "Regard my scheme not as the work of a spider to be crushed, but as the web that, with patience and labour, will snare the Trojans. Help me. Offer advice. Let's work together to make this all too raw plan ripen and succeed."

Palamedes is stymied, as are Ajax and Calchas.

But my moment doesn't last. Two guards drag a hobbled man into the light. This threesome is led by Iolochus, who belongs to Palamedes. Iolochus resembles some barbarian from the northern forests. His black beard runs up over his cheekbones to his very eyes, while his hairline cuts so low across his forehead that it nearly meets his brows. The hair in his ears is long enough to braid, while his chest is a rug, and even his back is thick with fur. Sinon has often mused that Iolochus is a not man at all but a species of badger, a beast from a cave. But no one doubts that he's dangerous, that his mind is a jaw, his opinions teeth, and everyone knows to keep their distance. These new arrivals halt at the edge of the firelight. "Agamemnon. Lord," calls Iolochus a little too loudly, a bit theatrically, trying to milk his entrance, his moment at centre stage. He has a strangely nasal voice, as if something has got lodged up in his nose. "I've caught another one. Urging desertion. I heard him myself," he adds, proudly, as if hearing is an accomplishment in and of itself. And given the thickets of hair in his ears maybe it is.

The prisoner tries to argue, but one of the guards twists the rope around the man's throat and he drops to his knees, head down. For the past year Iolochus has been weeding out dissenters; this poor bugger is the second this month, more evidence of disaffection.

Agamemnon asks the man if the charge is true.

The rope is tugged as if he is a dog being taught tricks. The fellow raises his bowed head exposing his face to the firelight: Dercynus. Half strangled, his eyes—one brown and one blue—swell horribly and his mouth gapes.

"Iolochus! Set him loose." He hesitates. I draw my knife and step forward.

"Iol'," says Palamedes finally and Iolochus frees Dercynus.

"Dercynus is as loyal as Palamedes," I say.

But the badger Iolochus disagrees in a tone gilded with sarcasm. "Pardon, Lord Odysseus. I heard him."

"With all that fur clogging your ears?" This earns un-easy laughter. His hair makes him the butt of jokes, though rarely are these spoken to his face. Iolochus's eyes survey the faces around the fire as if making note of the laughers while Palamedes, feigning amusement, drinks off his wine and sig-nals for more.

I repeat my question, "*You* or some *other* heard him?"

Iolochus glances once at Palamedes and then stands taller. "I."

I turn to Dercynus and ask what he has to say.

With his rope-ruined throat the best he can manage is a croak of denial.

Iolochus now claims he has witnesses, and even be-fore I can demand that he bring them forward, three men ad-vance from the shadows where they've been waiting, and all three echo the accusation: Dercynus urged mutiny.

"Those eyes of his say it all," says Iolochus. "They're not right. He's a betrayer. He looks in different directions at once. To Troy and to Greece."

"This is a dim argument even by your standards, Iolochus. What does all that hair say about you? That you're part rat?"

"He has witnesses," says Agamemnon. And, believing he has no recourse, he reluctantly gives the order: "His tongue."

And with no more ceremony than that, Dercynus is hauled off for amputation. "Agamemnon!" I clap my hands once, twice, a third time, as if the whole thing was theatre, a bit of farce, and that it's now time to be serious. I congratulate him on being a reasonable leader and wise judge, and yet also a man of sympathy, with a large mind and patient heart, and ask him to wait a little.

He's tired and frustrated, but he came to me to convince Achilles to return to the battle, and to me he'd come to solve the war: he owes me this much. He tells the guards to stop.

"Three witnesses?" I laugh scornfully. "You mean three paid perjurers. Give me a day, an hour, and I'll find ten men who'll vouch for Dercynus."

"Why should Iolochus lie?" asks Agamemnon.

"What's a ratter that fails to catch rats but a useless dog?"

Seeing victory about to slip away, Palamedes says, "Iolochus is not so quick to condemn as Odysseus suggests. I've been warned and I've been watching. I see the way this Dercynus hovers and whispers. I've heard his talk."

"Talk? You talk, Palamedes, almost as much as I do. Tonight we've heard Ajax and Calchas talk. We're Achaeans. We all talk. We never shut up," I add, glancing around to gather in the others, hoping to ease the atmosphere and pass this all off as an absurd lapse, a silly misunderstanding. "If we could get Priam and his generals out here around the fire we could talk them to death and never dirty our spears."

Palamedes puts on the sincere eye and speaks with an admiral façade of conviction. "But Odysseus. We enjoy hearing you talk. All your jokes and stories, your whimsies. Such an imagination, such a vocabulary, such poetry." Palamedes traces an arc with his hand and then pauses just long enough for everyone to savour the spice of his sarcasm. "Yet Dercynus . . . he talks differently. He talks treason. Besides, he'll fight as well without his tongue, maybe better."

Agamemnon looks to me with an expression that says Palamedes is right, an expression meant to remind me that Palamedes is a king, one of the grandsons of Poseidon, and his word is worth more than that of a mere soldier. He nods to the guards.

"Agamemnon. Let him go or I take my men and my ships home. You can finish your war by yourselves."

At this, Agamemnon shuts his eyes, pinches the bridge of his nose between his thumb and forefinger and exhales a long and exhausted breath.

Palamedes is quick to intervene. He inclines his head and smiles as if to say he understands the noble urges at work, but he must set me straight. "You're not Achilles, Odysseus. And justice must be done. It sets a bad precedent otherwise. There will be chaos."

I ignore him. It isn't Palamedes's decision, but Agamemnon's. Iolochus, the two guards, Dercynus, all of us, wait. The torches burn. The fire hisses. The bats tumble above us feeding on the mosquitoes while the waves shush quietly over the sand as if Poseidon is listening. Finally, with yet another enormous sigh, Agamemnon leans forward and rests one elbow on the carved arm of his cedar chair and wearily, sadly, but doggedly, regards me. "I'll kill any man who tries leaving this camp. Do you understand? King or boy, I'll kill him. If Menelaus tries to leave, I'll kill him."

From the corner of my eye I see that Menelaus doesn't so much as flicker at being included in this threat, as if he expects nothing less from his elder brother.

Agamemnon is bigger than me, and in a dead lift stronger, but he's also older and slower, so I rate my chances reasonably high that I can drop him. I took down Ajax, I'll take down this bearish ungrateful old Spartan. Yet what then? I can't just sail off. Menelaus won't stand for that. He'll be on me as soon as Agamemnon is dead. And it isn't likely I'll get out of a scrap with Agamemnon uninjured. I'll be hurt, perhaps badly, meaning Menelaus will have that much more advantage. Palamedes will be there taking bets, offering odds. Ajax will wager against me, eager to see me defeated. So, it seems to be my life versus Dercynus's tongue.

Agamemnon sighs back in his chair and Dercynus is led away into the night. I remain standing, sweat seeping down my brow and burning my eyes—eyes that have never before witnessed much less been the victim of such ingratitude. When Achilles threatened to leave I talked him into staying. When Agamemnon tested the army's will by lying that he'd had a Dream from Zeus telling us to sail home, the men ran to their ships eager to be off. I went among them and convinced them to stay and fight. Me. Odysseus. When Thersites ridiculed Agamemnon and encouraged everyone to run I beat him right there in public until he wept. Then I mastered the men so that they streamed back eager to fight. And this is my reward, this is the way of the mighty Agamemnon.

After a long silence, Agamemnon pitches his wine dregs hissing into the coals. The light trembles in the mother-of-pearl inlay of his chair, and his movement stirs the scent of the orange oil his boy rubs on him. "Time's running out," he says, opting now for a soft and coaxing tone. "Frustration, fatigue, and hunger are turning us against ourselves. Exactly what Priam wants. The Trojans have their city and their wells never run dry." His eyes urge me to see it from his perspective and consider the greater picture. In the firelight his beard looks carved in cave stone and his gaze is formidable. Still, I see now, more than ever, that he is a small king, without mercy, more interested in reputation than in the lives of his people. He has demonstrated this before. But now I see what little sway I have with him. Fine. A lesson learned, one I'll never forget. *Never again will I respect you, Agamemnon. You are a king all too familiar with the blood of your own men, worse, the blood of your own daughter, for it's all over your hands.*

But now he's eager to move us on by this unpleasantness. He wants to assuage me. "It must be a magnificent horse," he says smiling, trying to rekindle my enthusiasm, as if threatening me with death and cutting poor Dercynus's tongue out are quibbles not to be dwelt upon. "A horse the gods would envy," he says. "Jewels for eyes. Ivory for teeth. Beaten gold for hide. Only splendour will convince the Trojans," he adds, in case I might not know how the Trojans think. He then makes a performance of unscrewing the gold rings from each of his thumbs and drops them into his gold wine bowl. He adds the ruby that hangs from the chain around his neck. With that he passes the bowl on and every-one does likewise, until it's heaped as full as a basket of grapes at the harvest. Echion, excited at the prospect of the wooden horse, thrilled that something new is finally taking place, eager to participate, strips off every bit of metal he wears and adds it to the heap. Even Palamedes contributes a gold arm band fashioned like two twined serpents. I give the gold bracelets I took off the Trojan who kicked me in the knee. Only Ajax is blatantly reluctant, glowering as he gives his rings, but the example has been set by Agamemnon and can't be ignored. The horse will be built and it will be as splendid as the pyramids.

As the gathering disbands Menelaus appears at my side. He's been more than usually silent throughout the eve-ning. And yet I see by his troubled eyes that he's been think-ing. "It's a good plan, Odysseus. A good plan." He is adamant, his voice tense. We stand ten yards from the fire, the flame shadows slithering over the ground, a high haze veiling the moon. I want to ask why he left Paris alone with his wife and brought all this down on our heads. He reads the question in my eyes and is sorrowful. "She is everything you have ever imagined," he says.

He turns and walks away, head thrust forward, shoul-ders rounded under the weight of guilt.

*

I visit Dercynus. They've cleaned him up but he looks dreadful, pale, unconscious, breathing in spasms. Machaon says he dosed him heavily beforehand with poppy and wine. Tears nettle my eyes. "Is he going to live?" When Machaon starts in about 'the gods willing' I cut him off. "Don't give me that. Save him." I return to my tent fearing the dreams in store for me.

I don't dream as much as Penelope—who every morning had epics to relate—but my brain does its fair share of nocturnal churning. (I sometimes wonder if the world we call waking is in fact sleep for our world of dreams. When I suggested this to Penelope she looked at me as though I was a talking chicken.) I've gazed down upon armies as if a creature of the air, swum with dolphins, talked the language of ravens. For many years I've had a recurring dream about an egg. In it the yolk is the sun. And this sun hatches into a boy, only the hatching is an explosion, the shell and the gluten bursting, and the boy stands grown, a man holding a shield and gripping a spear, a crest of cock feathers atop his helmet of leather and brass, and with a shout he hurls the spear into the sky. It's a splendid throw, and the spear travels a day and a night, and pierces the sun. Only once again the sun is an egg yolk, and when the spear strikes it the yolk explodes, and the scenario begins all over.

But on this night I walk among mutes. They cling, grope, point east, point west, open their tongueless mouths which become caves leading down and down into the Underworld, where Hades waits on his throne of skulls . . .

I wake. It's long before dawn and my head is a stone. Staggering out for air I go immediately to check on Dercynus. He breathes shallowly, dried blood crusting his

mouth. To watch a man sleep is to know the terror of ultimate vulnerability. I kneel and whisper into his ear. "Valour,
son, valour. It's too soon to let go." I grip his hand and, to my
joy he returns the pressure.

At this hour the fires have burned low and the air is
cool. I return to my tent and lay on my back, taking reassurance in the weight of my forearm across my brow. Is it
possible that my other son, my blood son, Telemachus, is
dreaming of me right now? Is Penelope? I want to reach
through to her, to both of them, plunge my arm through a
waterfall and find their waiting hands. Sometimes I feel our
life together continues uninterrupted like a subterranean
stream, and yet all too often it seems as if we are dead to each
other, as if that stream has dried up.

When my grandfather, Autolycus, died I thought I
had lost my real father. For while Laertes was off with Jason
and the Argonauts chasing a reputation, Autolycus showed
me how to box and use the bow and the spear. He was a
quirky old man, full of songs and riddles, a notorious cattle
thief in his day, but he was devoted to me. He taught me the
constellations, said that Egyptians worshipped cats, Indians
worshipped cows, and that the northern barbarians dyed
themselves blue. It was he who took me on my first pig hunt.
We camped in the hills then drove the dogs down upon
them before sunrise, bursting through the mist like gods from
the clouds. The dogs had been muzzled all night and when
we unlocked their jaw-clamps their baying racketed between
the canyon walls. We cornered a boar. Huge and black with
curved tusks, it faced our spears in a snarling rage. We

stabbed at it from our horses and I found that I hated the beast because I feared it. At the same time I admired it the way I admired and hated a fire burning out of control. The horses tried trampling it. Their front legs pounded the air while their rear legs churned the dust. My grandfather dismounted. I did the same. Again and again we thrust our spears into the boar's neck. In its final panic it gored me, driving a tusk deep into my thigh before heaving me into the air. How clearly I remember that moment and still feel the hot stab of the tusk and how I flew, arms flailing, crying out like a hit bird.

Chapter Four

OVER THE NEXT few days I spend my time planning for the wooden horse and looking after Dercynus. I slaughter a goat and offer prayers but still he is bleeding. I dose Dercynus with poppy water and wine until he is so drunk he sings. Or tries. Without a tongue what a distorted song it is, a lament animal and otherworldly. Then I hold him as once again Machaon applies the cauterizing iron. Dercynus howls like a fate-cursed soul, and the only mercy is that between the agony and the poppy he passes out.

It's with guilty relief that I leave to meet with Epeius. He asks after the boy. I shrug and shake my head and we stand awhile in silence.

Epeius is one of those men who sees everything in the round, and can turn an image in his mind like a stone in his hand. He's also a master of siege-craft. After a suitable silence, he starts telling me that success in war can be traced to one principle: thrust, and the richest source of thrust is torsion.

"But," he cautions me, "it's also the most difficult to achieve, for it requires elasticity, and elasticity, Odysseus, elasticity is elusive, for it slackens, like a man's stomach." He grips a fold of his own belly which droops like a hag's dug. "Currently we use goat sinew, though I've had encouraging results with rope woven from horsehair. But," and here his voice grows intimate and he tilts his tall frame toward me, "I have an idea I know you'll appreciate: spider web. Yes. If it could be braided into cordage, well, you see the potential. Double maybe triple the range. Or up close, enough thrust to drive an arrow through a Trojan shield!" In demonstration, he shoots out a right jab.

I nod eagerly though I'm still not clear how this relates to the horse. When I ask him he is shocked.

"How?" His eyes darken with disappointment and he frowns, wondering how I can ask such a thing. "It all relates. If you could store torsion you could drive a wheel. Think of it, actually advance a cart without ox or horse." The strain must be showing on my face as I try envisioning what he's talking about. Frustrated, he makes as if to cuff me across the skull. "A cart, Odysseus. A chariot. A wooden horse. Anything with wheels. Think of a stone in a fire."

A stone in a fire? "All right. Yes." I'm with him so far.

"Think of the way it holds heat long after the coals have died."

I nod again. So far so good.

"If you could store thrust in the same way . . ."

"Like hate," I suggest, thinking of how it smoulders on in one's heart for days, even a lifetime.

"Hate? Yes, yes I suppose you could call it hate. Or rage."

"Latent power," I say slowly, the comprehension coming to a simmer in my brain.

"Exactly!" he shouts, gripping me by the shoulders and dancing.

We stroll arm-in-arm up and down the shore speculating upon torsion and spider webs and the heat stored in a stone, and most importantly, the construction of a colossal horse.

*

Dercynus dies and Machaon is resigned to punishment for failing to save him. I do nothing. What's the point? I ask if he regained consciousness or said anything? Machaon shakes his head. The corpse's face is chalk-white, the mouth twisted and the lips split. His hands, as if still prepared to fight, are clenched. We wrap him in a sheet soaked in eucalyptus.

Sinon and I bury him and then raise a modest mound set back in a discreet spot overlooking the sea. We pour blood and sing prayers and give him our best thoughts on his journey. As we look at each other over top of the mound, the fear in Sinon's eyes sparks fresh doubt in my heart. If I can't protect Dercynus, how can I expect Sinon to undertake the risk of letting himself be captured by the Trojans?

"Sinon," I begin, offering to let him withdraw from the scheme.

But he's ahead of me. He puts up his hand to block my words.

*

I am a cave to myself, warrened by ever-branching tunnels that lead not to epiphanies but to darkness. Gods? They're everywhere and in everything, but by that same token nowhere and in nothing. As unswayable as stones and as erratic as fire. Meaning? Meaning nothing. Riddle and paradox. Dercynus is dead and yet I sleep well. I actually wake refreshed and step out of my tent to see the sun grinding its invincible way up out of the land. On the first dawn following a funeral, no sight is crueller.

That day Epeius and I walk down the coast.

"Another grave mound," he says, meaning poor Dercynus.

The morning breeze gusts fresh off the sea. We find a tight cove with a smooth stretch of sand where, with his knife point, Epeius draws me a horse, in profile and plan and cross-section and three-quarter view, and we discuss issues of size and joinery and logistics.

"It has to be big," I caution. "With room inside for ten men. Plus water jars and a piss pot."

"And a spy hole out its eye," suggests Epeius. "You'll want to see what's going on."

"Yes. Exactly." His imagination has embraced the conceit and enlarged upon it. Talking to him always reminds me of how vast a man's mind can be, bigger than any palace, busier than any city, as full as the sea.

Then he's shaking his head as if he's made a mistake. "No, a spy hole won't be enough. It'll be too small. You'll have to use your ears. You'll have to listen. Hide stretched over a rib-work frame will be better than solid wood. And bunks," he adds, "for you could be stuck in there longer than expected."

I don't want to dwell on that possibility, but suppose it must be taken into consideration.

"Besides," he says, "lying down will allow you to wait more comfortably. You want to be rested when the moment comes."

I grow solemn and ask him what he really think of this horse idea.

He regards me as if taking my measurements, then he clears his throat and cocks his head to one side as if seeking the best words for the worst news. It's dangerous to ask for honesty, because what we really want is reassurance. He sighs and I grow wary, but at length he acknowledges that the horse has the merit of intrigue, and that intrigue is an excellent angle to have going for you. "The Trojans will have to be very wise or else as dull as cows to resist it."

"How long will it take to build?"

"You know the saying."

"I know a lot of sayings."

"Estimate your time," he says, "then double it."

I nod at such pragmatism.

"Right. First of all, the ship has to be beached then broken," he says. "That's the fun part. Allow five days. Then the more difficult business of actually building the horse: twenty days, though perhaps more. Then another five for transport by barge."

"Thirty days."

"Call it sixty."

"All right, sixty."

Epeius looks off now and narrows his eyes as if studying something in the distance. So convincing is he that I turn to look as well, but see only the pine trees and the burnt grass on the crumbling cliffs. He is nodding his head approvingly, as though he likes what he sees. He has pale grey eyes, a long nose, sparse hair and a small skull, proof that a big head does not mean a good brain. I've always liked him for he's calm and dignified and has wit. "It will be a horse as grave and beautiful as numbers," he concludes.

But which ship to break?

The question makes the rounds of the fire that night. Agamemnon looks to Calchas who calls for a cock and twists its neck. He pries open its breast with his thumbs as if splitting an orange and studies the viscera. He works his hands in its red and purple guts, sniffs his fingertips, gives them a lick and concludes that all the biremes uncaptained by death are ill-omened. This is a problem, because we can't very well take a ship out from under a Master who still lives. What to do? Good, kind, far-sighted Palamedes suggests a solution.

"Why doesn't Odysseus offer *his* ship? It's his scheme."

A murmur travels like a tremor through the assembly.

"There's beauty in this," admits Calchas innocently, as if he himself would never have thought of it, but now that the notion has been raised, well, as reasonable men, it's only prudent to give it due consideration.

"The goddess would approve," adds Palamedes, sounding solemn, though not even he can hide the joy in his glance, a glance that looks the way piss smells. All eyes are upon me.

"Fine. Excellent. My ship it is," I say brightly, as if honoured. "And while we're at it," I say. "I've been wondering about who should be in the horse. Me, naturally—"

The irrepressible Echion strains forward. "Me, Odysseus! And me!"

"Echion. Excellent. But give me a minute. Let's work down the list."

He slumps back.

"I'm thinking first of Palamedes and Ajax."

Pride drives Ajax to immediate acceptance.

"Good. Palamedes?" I look queryingly at him, convinced it's more prudent to have him in the horse than manipulating from afar. "Such a majestic warrior must of course be included in this most glorious of ventures. Think of it: Ajax, Menelaus, Diomedes, Palamedes and me, Odysseus. How can we fail? The ode masters will sing our glory. For a thousand years men will speak of us. For eternity the gods will recall the day Troy fell. It would be unfair to exclude one such as Palamedes."

In the silence that follows, the fire burns quieter and even the waves seem to cease their pounding as if they too listen. Eyes glittering like crushed glass, Palamedes spreads his arms wide as if to embrace me. "Much honour you do me, Odysseus. I thank you. And I accept."

Cups clash in a toast. Agamemnon appears content. Even Calchas relaxes. The relief is palpable, as if a breeze has cleared a corpse stench from under our noses. Much happy chatter follows, until Palamedes interjects with an afterthought, employing the cautionary tone of a prudent elder concerned for the safety of children.

"Brave Odysseus," he says, wrinkling his humble brow in innocent reflection. "Shrewdest of us all. Master in the Arts of War. Consider this: when one stands too close to a stone you cannot see that it is a part of a wall." By way of demonstration this wise counsellor, this brother-in-arms, holds his palm against his eyes. "Nor can you see that the wall is part of a house, and that the house may harbour an enemy. If I am not mistaken, I think you and I will agree that only distance and perspective give such knowledge."

I incline my head and put on the face of one eager for his wisdom.

"Therefore I'm only wondering, Odysseus, if you're not perhaps too close to your most excellent scheme," he says. "Blades, after all, are forged to the task. No one fells an oak with a cleaver, and no one cuts onions with an axe. So with warriors. They must be deployed where most fit."

"Immense is the wisdom of Lord Palamedes. He is right to correct me. A problem is indeed best viewed from all angles by many sets of eyes. An exploit such as this is a perilous one, and wise is he who knows whether his strength lies in his arms to fight or his legs to run."

I may as well have spat in his wine bowl for the stare he gives me.

"Speed is a valuable asset," I continue, innocent of any insinuation. "In the horse a fast runner would indeed be wasted. Or a great arm with a javelin. This will be a manoeuvre favouring men—" and here I hesitate a beat so that the word *men* should register "—favouring men who work best in close combat: sword and dagger, axe and fist." I began my little performance intending only to nettle him, but the further I go the angrier I become, because he was behind the framing of Dercynus, because he put the knife to my Telemachus's throat, because he is to blame for my wasting years here in this absurd war. So I push hard. "Your point being, Palamedes, that you're a—"

"My point being that I don't like small places and I don't like small men."

Everyone and every thing falls still. The air and the earth and the sea lay silent. Even the fire seems to cringe. And then a single blue spark pops and lands on Palamedes's bare knee. He doesn't flinch, he doesn't turn his gaze from me, he makes no move to brush away the burning ember. Perhaps he thinks it's a sign. No doubt old Couch Ass is already devising his interpretations.

At last Agamemnon slaps his thigh and announces that Palamedes would indeed be wasted in the horse. "He will stay by my side. That we may watch together for the burning arrows signalling the horse is inside Troy. And if the signal doesn't come," he adds, "I will need shrewd counsel." Is this an attempt to make amends for Dercynus? Or is he as suspicious of Palamedes as I am? Eager to move on to safer matters, Agamemnon now turns to Epeius, but Palamedes isn't finished.

"As would a man of Menelaus's stature," he observes quietly, soberly. "His very presence leading an army inspires the men and terrifies the enemy. Shut up in the horse that presence would be lost. Why keep such a flame in the dark?"

Palamedes knows Agamemnon will not abandon his brother, yet with me isolated Palamedes will happily see the horse burn. Thus he sacrifices Ajax but keeps a direct line to Agamemnon via Menelaus.

"No."

We all turn.

Menelaus. Standing. Breathing hard. "I have to reach her before Paris has a chance to take her away. He'll disappear with her. Into the East." He gestures indicating the deserts and mountains and marshes stretching away toward Persia.

I will give him that much, he has pride and he has boldness, and he wants his woman back. Even Palamedes is caught with his mouth open. Agamemnon, as if suddenly sick of the whole business, as if suddenly too old to bear a moping Menelaus, says fine, as you see fit. And so Ajax and Menelaus will join Diomedes and I in the horse.

*

That night I dream that suitors circle Penelope like randy cats, while others, subtle, smiling, befriend Telemachus, playing kick the pig's bladder with him, teaching him to box and wrestle and swim, the very things I should been doing. In the dream Penelope mourns me, but after ten years alone her heart begins to waver and she's ready to be swayed, for a son needs a father, and Odysseus—trapped, killed, cursed, or simply indifferent—has vanished over the sea . . .

I wake as desolate as I've been since leaving Ithaka. Tormented, I step out into the night and walk the beach. By now Telemachus has likely forgotten what I even look like. Would I recognise him?

When the midwife presented me my son wrapped in a wool blanket, I'd looked into a pair of deep green eyes that were already at work evaluating me, as if I was the one who had newly arrived, not him, as if I'd entered his world and not the other way around. And it seemed to me he was already reaching conclusions. I remember asking him what he thought and he merely gazed at me as if biding his time, as if implying that he'd wait awhile before letting me know. He wasn't disturbed in the least by my bearded face looming in upon him. I was relieved. In fact I felt honoured, the same as when a bird allows you to approach, for both are mysteries and it's a privilege to be allowed near.

Penelope worried that Helen would hear of the boy and decide to pay us a visit. Helen was Penelope's dark obsession. At times she sneered at the notion of Helen being the offspring of Zeus and Leda. At other times she did not doubt it. Penelope grew up with Helen and described flocks of swans wandering freely about the palace, fed upon the finest grain, the purest water. Anyone caught abusing them in any way, even so much as a harsh word, was whipped. Except Helen. She could get away with anything. She'd grip the biggest swan around the throat and climb onto its back demanding that it fly her up into the air. She'd pluck their feathers. Chase them. Leda said nothing. She indulged her. They all indulged her, the daughter of Zeus. Even I, in far off Ithaka, wanted to see the splendid Helen born of an egg.

Of everyone who went to Sparta only I arrived without a gift. No pearls grow on the shores of Ithaka, no rare woods on our hillsides, no gold lies in our stream beds, the craft of the weavers and potters is utilitarian at best. Besides, I didn't need a seer to predict she wouldn't be choosing an obscure prince from a small island, no matter what I might give.

There was a banquet in honour of the athletes come to impress Helen by running and jumping and wrestling like so many monkeys. I recall a marble-floored hall with pillars and iron lamp stands and caged ravens. There was so much food—roasted peacock, stuffed hens, braised dolphin, pork tongues, wolf brains, Chios wine, fig liqueur—that it was cruel, for anyone who ate and drank his fill would never make it out of bed the next morning much less be able to compete. Helen didn't make an entrance, there were no trumpets or drums or heralds making speeches—she appeared—silent, still, standing like white fire. Her hands were clasped before her as if she was there to serve, as though our comfort was paramount. She had remarkable hands, long and expressive, each finger a serpent capped with a red nail. She smiled a smile disconcertingly dark and cave-like, for it didn't show her teeth.

She wasn't beautiful. Striking, yes, beautiful no. She appeared differently to each of us. Menelaus saw the ideal woman, her features perfect in their symmetry, her manner regal, eyes calm, breasts neither too small nor too large, waist just so, ankles slim, none of your cow-hipped peasants with udders to feed a herd; a woman worthy of marble. Palamedes saw a delicate creature, small, demure, obedient, with down-cast eyes, her hair woven with gold threads and blood-drop rubies. Diomedes saw a night creature, her smile as seductive as moonlight on water, and with a notorious taste for oil and the lash. Ajax whispered of a creature as majestic as an eagle; I saw a woman lean and hard and feral, her face all planes and angles. A woman in a panic.

One thing we all agreed upon were her hands. Even Penelope used to talk about "the disposition" of Helen's fingers. It was as if her hands were puppets and she was always aware of what they were up to, languid or threatening, bored or curious. She'd often find Helen alone studying her fingers, posing them like a little crowd of dolls. She'd make Penelope play shadow puppets with her. Would want to play all night and got angry when Penelope grew tired, threatening her, hitting her, twisting her arm and pulling her hair or alter-nately pleading with her and giving her jewelry, anything to have a playmate.

But now Helen greeted us, spreading her arms wide as if she would embrace us all. She wore no rings or bracelets or bands, and her voice was low and full of the undertones of bronze. "Welcome."

Before anyone could rise she was drawing out her own chair. Even the serving boys seemed too entranced to act. Her gaze visited each of our faces. Did her eyes linger upon me? She certainly took a moment to regard smooth-faced young Ajax who was scarcely fourteen years old.

She sipped her wine and began asking the man to her right his name and that of his father and the story of his journey. In this manner she spoke to each of us, and we did our best to charm and impress, to capture that most illusive of all prizes, another's heart. How attentive she was, how complete and utter her focus. When she spoke to you, you were at the centre of the world, the centre of *her* world, which was the only one that mattered, and when she moved on to the next man you felt as if the sun had disappeared behind a cloud, that you'd been cast out to the dark regions of exile, and your foremost goal—your only goal—was to regain the radiance of Helen's attention. Ajax acquitted himself well.

"And would you marry me?" she asked him, her voice throaty with amusement but at the same time bearing about her brow a seriousness, as if this young man, this boy, genuinely intrigued her, and she would not be so callous as to insult him.

Gripping the table edge, Ajax stood and in a bold tone told her that he was by far the best choice, because when these old men were leaning on sticks, he would be young and vigorous.

She arched one eyebrow and had to agree that, seen in such a light, his youth was indeed an advantage, and thanking him she wished him fortune in the games.

My turn was approaching. I had a belly full of bees, for as well as having failed to bring a gift, I'd prepared no speech or story or clever reason why she should choose me before anyone else. The only thing I had to offer was exactly the same as the other men—my mortality, the fact that I would die—the one thing the daughter of Zeus would never experience. When my turn came I said, simply, teasingly, in the spirit of the evening, "In loving me you will taste the salt that gives this brief life its savour." And with that I smiled and was silent.

She said nothing for a moment, reflecting upon this, the briefest speech of the evening. Then she threw her head back and laughed so loudly she nearly blew out the torches. "But death is not unique to you, Odysseus. Every man here will die. Even the beautiful young Ajax." The way she spoke made it sound like a curse that it was in her power to declare or rescind. Could she bestow immortality on the man she chose? The question bloomed in the mind of every one of us; perhaps it had been there from the start, perhaps it was the very reason we were here at all, to lie with an offspring of the gods.

And then Helen was gone. A flame snuffed. How sudden it seemed, even though she'd thanked us again and wished us well. When she departed it was as though music had stopped, night had fallen, and the silence that remained was as desolate as dried bones on a beach.

And now, twenty years later, I could still feel that desolation right through the anger and resentment. I turned back, wishing for the hundredth time that I'd never gone to Sparta at all, though of course then I'd never have met Penelope. Irony within paradox. Something bad breeds something good, the flower in the cesspool.

*

Plodding back along the shore, I am shaken from these rec-
ollections of Sparta by shouting. I creep through the thorn-
scrub and find Palamedes and Iolochus backing young
Sinon against a pine tree. When I step forward Iolochus
runs at me with his sword until seeing who it is and hesitates.

Palamedes is all charm. No poisoned water ever slid
so smoothly over polished rock. "Odysseus. Excellent timing.
Your man here—" With his blade he indicates Sinon as if di-
recting my attention to the finer points of a slave. "He's a
brave one. Attacked us both, one against two."

I don't need to interrogate Sinon to know a lie.
Palamedes has it in mind to kill both of my aides. A nice pro-
ject. Knock the pins out from under Odysseus. "Yes, he's a
lively one. Young men. Erratic as spring winds. But they
pass," I add. "No harm done."

"Oh," says Palamedes in a tone almost sprightly, "but
harm has been done." He shows me a blood-stain on his robe
between his hip and ribs.

"My blade's clean," argues Sinon.

"Show us," says Palamedes.

Sinon raises his sword—coated in dark blood. By his
expression I could very well think he's the one who's been
dirked. I'm frankly impressed. Had Sinon thought he was doing me a favour by killing Palamedes? "Palamedes," I say,
making with the sincere voice, "Let me have a look at that
wound."

He jumps back as if scalded. "You and yours have done enough, Odysseus. My wound, like my life, is my own." And in one swift swing he catches Sinon across the upper arm. The boy cries out and drops. Palamedes raises his blade again but I block it with my own. The reverberation of the strike runs down through my elbow. Now Iolochus manoeuvres to get at Sinon, but I drop to a crouch and slash him across the calf. I feel the tendons split; he'll never walk straight again if he walks at all. Palamedes sheaths his sword, raises his hand in a curious little gesture typical of him, half wave and half insult, maybe part incantation too, something picked up from Calchas, and withdraws into the night.

I tie Sinon's arm and hurry him back to Machaon, because Palamedes is a great one for wiping his blades in shit or venom. Iolochus we leave groaning in the dirt. It's tempting to break a few of his ribs for good measure, maybe put my heel in and snap his collarbones, and then as a finishing touch, cut out his tongue and whisper in his ear that Dercynus says hello. It's what he deserves. I've often watched Iolochus perform Nauplian folk dances, curious as to how his apelike face grows reflective and almost refined. There'll be no more dancing for him.

Machaon rubs Sinon's wound with crushed garlic, the boy protesting his innocence the entire time until I assure him I know old blood from fresh. "You'd better keep a closer eye on your weapons," I advise him. "What were you doing out there in the middle of the night?"

"Following you."

Touched by such loyalty, I mask the spasm of emotion by telling him he'd better heal quickly for he's the only one I trust to do a good job plucking my ears.

Chapter Five

THE NEXT HIGH TIDE we lock hawsers onto bulk-heads, draw up anchor stones, and twenty men drag my blue-prowed ship onto the beach, her keel shrieking against the gravel. The shipwrights are terrifying to watch. One day and they take up her decking, and in three all that remain are keel and ribs, a whale picked to the bone. I love that ship. I've often gone aboard her and sat with my back to Troy and my face to the sea, recalling the rhythm of the oars and the moan of the planks. I should be home teaching Telemachus to sail. Epeius sees my expression and steps to my side and reminds me that there are other ships in the fleet, I can take my pick. Nonetheless I call for one of the oars, stout oak, and order it kept aside. I wink at Epeius and say I'll take it home and plant it on the hill above my house and grow a new ship, for my son.

He likes that.

Men posted in the hills keep the Trojans from seeing what we're doing. I want the horse discovered only after we've burned our camp and the fleet has set sail for Tenedos. Let the horse appear as suddenly as Helen had appeared that night in Sparta. The metamorphosis from ship to horse intrigues me. I set up a tent alongside that of Epeius and remain on-site. A fifty-oared bireme will become an animal three poles high at the shoulder, the curved hull planks the hindquarters, the deck-wood the legs, the rendered feet of our dead cattle the glue, and their tails plaited into a mane. Everyone has suggestions. Carbuncle eyes, a tail of lion hair, a skin made of stitched horsehide stamped with gold, a whalebone saddle, stirrups of bronze.

Epeius, Diomedes, and I spend entire days overseeing the work. The smiths fuel their forges and hammer out bolts and plates and pins observed by statues of their crippled god Hephaestus.

"The ancients thought iron fell from the sky," I say.

"Fish have noses," says Diomedes, apropos of nothing. "But can they smell?"

"They sometimes stink."

"Watch," he says, and stands on one foot with his arms folded like wings. "A goose."

"Excellent," I say. "That'll come in handy."

Epeius and I exchange glances.

"The full moon," I say, explaining his oddness. Returning to the topic of metal, I recount the story of how, on the road to Sparta, a hermit took me for a robber and decided to finish me off before I could do any more robbering. He charged me with a sword even more ancient than he was, made of the old iron, the blade softer than gold. I side-stepped the blow, which hit the ground bending the blade sideways, so that it was as cocked as a dog's hind leg. The old warrior used his foot to straighten the bend while I drew my own sword and swatted him across the butt with the flat of my blade.

"And you became great friends?" mocks Diomedes.

"No. He tried kneeing me in the balls."

Epeius observes that if we could find a metal as light as wood but as strong as brass our infantry would be as invincible as the gods.

I ask him if he's ever seen a god.

Before he can respond Diomedes announces that he wants to kill one.

"One what?"

"One god."

"Ah." I nod politely and ask him how he proposes to do this. I love and admire Diomedes and find him endlessly intriguing even when he's being an ass.

Adopting the sober tone of a practical man, he admits it won't be easy, as if I'm the one who needs reminding that the gods are immortal. We fall into a discussion as to how best to achieve this curious goal of his. Mulling the problem, we eliminate poison and knives and spears and arrows and hammers. I suggest that perhaps he can trick one god into killing another . . .

Diomedes brightens. He waggles a finger at me meaning I've hit upon an interesting possibility. Then he falls glum. "I'm not that clever."

"You just want to cosh one on the head."

He indignantly denies this. He insists that he has a grander vision and paints the scene for us. "An arena. An audience. Flowers. Poets. A fair fight witnessed by all."

And a reputation that will last forever, I think, you who are always mocking the pursuit of fame. I don't mention this, however. Instead I inquire as to whether he has any god in particular in mind.

He looks at me as if the answer is obvious. "Ares."

The master of war . . . I begin to see his larger motivation. Kill him and kill war itself. A noble aim. A gesture I envy, a gesture I admire. As ever, I'm impressed by the man. Charmed, in fact. Still, I'm sceptical. How can a man kill a god? And if it is possible, by some trick, by some spell, the gods would take revenge, for it would be a precedent and soon they'd have nothing but insolent men on their hands. Apparently my face betrays these doubts.

Diomedes grows impatient. He says it is symbolic. "Even a wound would do. Something to drive Ares off the field." He turns to Epeius for his approval.

Epeius has remained silent all this time, bemused by our antics. He suggests, in his considered fashion, that fate has a face, and it is a grimly ironic one, and that gods are one expression of that dark wit. "Seers are another."

"Exactly," cries Diomedes. "I've always said Calchas is a joke."

I recall one so-called seer who made it across the strait to Ithaka. He had a gibbled foot, a long beard, bald head, and his front teeth were gone so his words were slush. I had Telemachus with me. He was about three at the time. The stranger said he'd tell the boy's fate, all he needed was a goat and a fire. I laughed at him. He said okay, a hen and a fire. So we built up the coals and I sent for a hen. Why not? A little diversion on a grey day. It was winter; a hard wind sloping in off the sea. The hen was scrawny. The worst of the flock. The seer was disappointed but said nothing, just pulled off the bird's head as if plucking a cork from a jug. Telemachus looked at me, blinking, not sure what had just happened, because he liked chickens and the sight of killing upset him. The seer slipped the head into his pocket. Maybe he considered it a delicacy or perhaps he'd use the beak as a whistle. I don't know. He gripped the carcass in both hands as if squeezing a wine skin and out squirted a string of blood. I half expected him to read the red scribble on the sand but he ignored it, and instead set about pluck-ing and gutting the bird and then positioning it over the coals. He added salt from a pouch. He cut up a lemon and squeezed the juice onto the meat. A very attentive cook, this man, prodding and turning the bird with a knife so that it didn't burn. Finally he ate it, squatting there on his heels, chewing the meat, sucking the neck bones, licking his fin-gers. Then he belched and snugged up the salt pouch and put it away in his pocket, cleaned his hands with the last of the lemon and prepared to leave. I was smiling now, curious about the old scammer. He'd pulled one over on me, so I reminded him about reading Telemachus's fate. "And my son's future?"

"Oh, a long one," he said, "very long, but as lean as this bird."

*

As the horse progresses even the doubters grow enthused. Menelaus and Agamemnon wear the grins of boys; Palamedes is politely observant; Iolochus hobbles past on his crutch and spits. Among the men the horse is the sole topic of conversation. Only Ajax is indifferent. He ignores it completely despite the fact that he too will take his place inside it. Instead he begins acting erratically, forgetting to wash, talking to himself, vanishing for days at a time. I start to worry. Do I want this man in the horse with me? I ask Sinon to watch him.

Sinon usually sleeps outside my tent. At dawn the very next morning, while I'm still in bed, he positions himself just inside the flap so he can observe Ajax, whose tent is directly opposite. As he sits there, Sinon casually unwraps Achilles's armour and begins polishing it, a common enough task for him, but this morning there is something different about the way he goes about it, an element of the actor is at work as he fawns over each piece, as if it were his very own. Each time I see the armour I'm impressed. Ajax is right to covet it. Hephaestus fashioned it for Achilles at the request of Thetis. It seems almost to breathe like a bronze skin. The gift of a god to a half-god.

As if the armour calls out to him, Ajax stirs and sits up. Sinon opens the flap wider, exposing the armour to plain view. As the sun rises the armour fairly shouts with an unavoidable radiance, and it is the first thing Ajax sees. Working diligently with rag and oil, Sinon pretends to be unaware of being watched. He whistles softly, the high tone shaped by the smile curling his lips. His impersonations have always bordered upon the cruel. The very source of their brilliance is his attention to detail, keen, accurate, merciless. He delights in his art. Is more alive when in *persona*, as he is now, pretending to be but a simple soldier absorbed in a routine task. I freely admit that I love Sinon. He is a son to me. He is the boy who was nearly killed by Palamedes and Iolochus while trying to protect me. But there is no denying that he savours the pain of others with a little too much relish. Ajax has never given him so much as a bad word. Dercynus was not so clever but he was kinder, perhaps wiser. I ask him if he has urinated long enough on Ajax's wounds?

Sinon promptly wraps up the armour. The tilt of his head expresses the sting and indignation of the unjustly rebuked. I remind him that I'd asked him to watch Ajax, not torment him.

Ajax, meanwhile, has left his tent and vanished.

*

Eager to redeem himself, Sinon is back by mid-afternoon reporting that Ajax has begun to spurn Palamedes. Intrigued, I set aside the wax plugs I was about to fit into my ears before settling in for a nap. I stand. I pace the tent, questioning Sinon closely. I'm inspired to make another attempt at reconciliation. In the stores taken off my ship I discovered one last pot of wildflower honey, and the next dawn, while Ajax slips from the camp on one of his wanders, I call out to him. He averts his face and hunches his shoulders as if he doesn't want to hear, as if I am a cold wind. But I mean to settle this before getting myself sealed up inside the horse with a man who hates me even more than he hates the Trojans. We walk in silence until we are beyond the camp and the stables, the sun warming the land while the sandpipers flee at our approach. I show him the honey.

He hardly glances at it, just lengthens his stride and walks faster. Reaching a rocky point we wade waist-deep into the water to round it, the sand swirling about my feet, shards of shell lodging between my sandal and sole. Holding the honey pot in one arm and balancing with the other, I suddenly wallow and grow fearful at how easy it would be for Ajax to simply turn and drown me.

"I once looked to you as a father," he announces as we regain dry land. His voice is breezy, as if referring to some fondly recalled stranger. "Sought your counsel. Confessed my fears. And you gave me riddles." He sounds bemused, almost chuckles. I run to catch up, the soft sand sucking at my sandals, my bad knee throbbing. "When I failed to solve the riddles you gave me scorn." Only now does he look at me, long hair knotted with twigs, upper lip unshaved, glance clawing me with the tethered rage of a betrayed dog. He raises his forefinger as if expecting me to interrupt. "Scorn," he repeats. "Honeyed with pleasantries. Sweet thorns whose prick you thought I was too dull to feel. No," he says, seeing my surprise. "I'm not always stumble-tongued. And you, you're not as subtle as you think you are."

So, this is how he remembers those days. Is he right? My wit is dry and my jokes too often taken for insults. Even

Penelope, who knows me best, sometimes grew teary at some quip or sarcasm, however innocently intended.

The first time I saw Ajax he'd just caught a moth and had it cupped in his hands as if holding water. He was standing outside the athletes' tent, so absorbed by the moth that I was able to step right up behind him undetected. He was gazing at it as if he'd never seen such a miracle. I'd only just arrived in Sparta, the new moon a sickle and torches maddening the insects. He was the first person I spoke to. "Do you remember the Death's Head Moth?" I ask him now.

Ajax slows at this and grows defensive. "You thought I was absurd. A child. A collector of bugs."

Not true. Or only partly. I was also charmed. "I was impressed, Ajax. You, fourteen years old, travelling all the way to Sparta on your own. That took guts, more mettle than some grown men ever show. But I'll tell you one thing, every man there was fearful when they saw you compete."

He shakes his head. He isn't going to be so easily flattered a second time. "Always side-smiling and smirking at me."

I admit I'd smirked and grinned along with the other athletes at the spectacle of this earnest boy so eager to win the prize. There he was, splendid and absurd, never having touched a girl much less grasped any notion of his mortality. The first day he practised with a javelin that was almost as thick as his arm. I had to wonder at his father, Telamon, permitting his son to chase such a fantasy. Was it a lesson in the school of hard knocks? A dose of the real world for a boy reared in a palace?

"You did well," I remind him now as I follow along the shore with the honey like some market tout dogging a customer.

"I lost."

"I lost, too."

"You quit."

To Ajax there is no greater humiliation. I try to argue but his mind is off on its own memories. "Do you recall telling me about the mad honey of Trebizond?" he asks.

"Of course."

He smiles the smile of a thousand-year-old man adrift upon the mornings of his youth. He angles his way up the beach to where dry grass tufts amid the rocks. "I liked that story," he says, fond now. "Rhododendron honey. With a bee god in it. I wanted to taste it. I'd have risked the madness for a taste. Didn't you ever wonder what it was like?" He halts so suddenly that I nearly bump into him. He gazes at me with the open expression he'd so often worn in those early days. He was the age then that my Telemachus is now. Would a braver man have simply refused to join this absurd siege; would a wiser man have shrugged and simply told Menelaus no, I won't go, instead of pretending to be mad? I could have risked his anger, endured the shame of breaking my vow, explained to my boy that, unlike my own father, it was more important for me to stay and see him grow up. Instead, ten years have been lost, my reputation remains uncertain, my son doesn't know me and my wife has no idea whether I am alive or dead.

"The taste of that honey has to be—" His vocabulary fails him and he shakes his head. "I thought you must be lying, but Nestor—a wise man, well-travelled, honest—he knew of it, a lot of men did. But I'll never taste it. Not now." When I ask why, he responds sarcastically. "It was a Death's Head Moth, Odysseus. I won't last long here. Hades has his eye on me. I can feel it. You think what you want, but I know what I know."

A creature of instinct, Ajax, so optimistic as a boy, so grim as a man. The most loyal of us all, believing in the honour of this war, but he needs someone or something to be loyal to, except everyone has failed him: his own father the great Telamon, me, and perhaps most of all Agamemnon, who cheated Achilles and let the war drag on.

The land rises and soft sand gives way to packed dirt. Wind-bent pines lean like a gathering of cripples to watch our passing. I break the wax seal on the honey, yet Ajax regards it as if peering into a suspect well. "Too little, too late." Not deigning to even dip his finger and taste it, he strides on, his hands clasped philosopher-wise behind his back.

I call, "I've been thinking. You'd be wasted in the horse."

This halts him with the suddenness of a stallion whose reins have been jerked. He tosses his head and laughs loudly, scornfully, as if expecting as much, as if this is all too typical of two-faced Odysseus and his sly tactics, and then he walks on, and I'm left standing there with a pot of honey already crawling with flies despite the hot wind blowing in off the glittering sea. I wander back down the slope to the beach and sit in the shade of a stone. I'd talked Achilles into staying and fighting when he'd announced he was leaving, but Ajax has walled up his ears. To him I have no honour. I look into the honey's dim gold depths as if expecting to read some omen—hoping for once to see the splendid Athena—but find nothing but bits of twig and leaf and the wing of a dragonfly.

*

In the days that follow, Ajax begins to drink, not just wine but wormwood, and his mind veers so that he rages at everything and everyone, stabbing the air at ghosts and phantoms, no longer bothering to take himself off in decorous exile, but going mad in plain view. Clothes piss-rank and filthy, he reels in front of my tent calling me out, telling me to put on Achilles's armour and give us all a show. "A dwarf in giant's bronze!" I try talking to him but he can only repeat that I cheated in the games for the armour, that I have the honour of a dog, and that in time men will sing songs of scorn about me. "You have more faces than a dog has hairs. Keep your prize, Odysseus. But remember—it will always be too big for you."

Agamemnon tries talking to Ajax, putting his arm around his shoulders and painting pictures of glory, speaking of prizes and home and, above all, of reputation, of the respect of his father Telamon who had been one of the Argonauts and fought alongside Herakles and Jason, but Ajax's ears remain shut. The time for prizes and listening is over. As for lesser men, Ajax cuffs them aside when they try reasoning with him; he even tells Calchas to go shove his head up a bull's ass and read its guts.

Once in Sparta I watched the young Ajax lying in a field studying bees. He enjoyed the sensation of them walking on his fingers, and they never stung him, something that pleased him immensely, something that made him proud, as if he'd won their confidence, as if he was as sweet as the flowers themselves. I can easily imagine Telemachus doing the same.

Chapter Six

THE HORSE IS COMPLETE except for the eyes. Eyes will give the illusion of life even to a wooden animal, as if some spark of Soul has been lured to fly down and inhabit it. Lengthy discussions take place on how best to make them. Every combination of pearl and ruby, amethyst and shell, silver and gold and bronze are suggested. Epeius considers candles behind glass but is stymied by the problem of smoke. I suggest fireflies, we catch some but they refuse to glow in captivity and the philosophers among us speculate on the relationship between liberty and light. What about obsidian and silver? White marble overlaid with sapphires? The discussion continues, everyone taking part except for Ajax.

Ajax no longer talks to anyone. Like the wasps of the waning summer, he has grown sluggish and stumbling and withdrawn. We are all anxious. We all worry. The very possibility that we could soon be going home causes fear, as if regardless of all the years and the frustration, the sweat and blood and loss, it's suddenly happening too soon, but Ajax is troubled beyond all this.

One morning I rise earlier than usual and swim in the sea, floating on my back and watching the stars dim and the sky brighten. Then I walk through the camp. The dogs paw the cold ashes for bones and the ravens caw in the pines. Dogs are useful creatures, like hens and goats, yet I've always preferred cats. Dogs slobber and stink while cats have the dignity to groom themselves. They arrange their kills in a row, heads pointing in the same direction, an admirable display of symmetry that also appeals to me, though I can see the tedium of too much order. A little chaos, a little disarray, has the charm of children. And yet such thoughts make me nostalgic, and with nostalgia comes regret, an enervating indulgence to which I'm growing all too prone, another reason I admire cats, they seem impervious to self-doubt.

The farther I walk inland the heavier the dew and the mist. These are the grasslands where our horses pasture and I expect to hear the meditative sounds of grazing. Instead I hear the shriek of panicked animals, the wet chop of a blade striking meat. There. Ajax. In the dragging mist he lunges with his sword, battling not men but horses, the very last of our mounts. In his spiralling dementia the animals are Trojans. "Ajax!" He staggers on gore-slick grass and looks around, groggy, confused, as if waking, and sees his work: a slaughterhouse of heaving animals writhing and coughing blood. More painfully, he sees what he's been reduced to. He, second only to Achilles, he, the one with the greatest faith in our cause. I shout again, but he turns his blade upon himself and, arms fully extended, blade pointing inward, grips the sword with both hands. He fixes his gaze on me—a gaze that lasts half a heartbeat but bears the weight of a lifetime with all its hope and lament and accusation—and pulls death into his heart. Dropping to his knees he topples forward driving the blade through his chest and out his back. He lies face down in the grass, the protruding blade gleaming wet in the newly risen sun whose heat breathes warmly, mockingly, over my face. Is this the laughter of the sun god? Is this a lesson to be learned? First Dercynus, now Ajax. The cawing ravens flee from the trees. I run slipping in the blood, and when I reach him the flies are already at work. Ajax lies in a small cluster of blue flowers. I roll him onto his back so that he might feel the sun on his face one last time, but his Soul has already departed. My head falls back and I would cry out if I had the strength but there is nothing in me. When I open my eyes, I see that the branches above me drip with blood.

*

How strangely ancient Ajax looks in death, his stomach concave, skull gaunt, his fingers curled like claws, the nails so thoroughly chewed they're painful to look at. I recognize each of his scars. A man's body grows ever more distinct as it ages, bent and stunted by the life it has endured. With the help of Diomedes and Menelaus we lift the corpse onto a cypress litter while all of us, Athenians, Spartans, Cephallonians, Myceaneans, walk past with bowed heads offering our respects. Sinon too has the decency to show remorse, perhaps even genuinely feel it. Lacking women to keen, the men groan aloud like a chorus of bulls and strike their chests until the dogs begin to howl. Palamedes whispers to both Agamemnon and Menelaus and I know I'm being blamed. It's easy to kindle suspicion in an Achaean. It's a chronic flaw in our character. Like fire in a peat bog, suspicion smoulders on beneath the surface, and Palamedes fans the coals.

It's a bad omen for a man like Ajax to kill himself. It worries the men, they begin to murmur. *Where were the gods that love him? Why did one not whisper in his ear? What does this mean? We should have left long ago when we had the chance . . .* I'm not immune to these very same questions, but anyone who knew Ajax will attest to the obsessive intensity that consumed him from within, a mortal striving vainly for immortality.

We bury Ajax on a hill looking westward over the sea. Masons polish the stones that line his tomb. His finest war axe and the sword he won from Hector accompany him. There are no more bulls to sacrifice so we lead his two best stallions to the mound, soothing their anxiety for they sense the knife even though I hide it behind my back as I whisper of barley and clover. I stand between them, my head alongside their necks, and for a time we remain that way until their breathing settles and their heartbeats slow and the flies return. Then I slit their throats. As their forelegs buckle I continue whispering of apple orchards and rich fields of sweet clover. We leave a tunnel to the open door of his crypt so that Ajax can watch the games we hold in his honour. Before we bolt the bronze hasps on the coffin and fill the tunnel, I retrieve Achilles's damned armour and place it in the tomb. Let Ajax wear it on his final journey. The gleam of the bronze will light his way. Hades will rise from his throne of skulls and welcome him.

Inescapably we discuss what we all know and fear—that the Trojans will take advantage of our loss and strike while we're grieving, exactly what we would do to them. We have to act. Calchas argues that time is needed for sacrifices, Agamemnon reminds him that there is nothing left to sacrifice.

"We move now."

Everyone looks to Epeius, who smiles and announces that the horse is ready.

*

It stands three poles from hoof to ear and every one of us thinks we should bring it home instead of Helen. Bronze hooves, red amethyst eyes ringed with green beryls, ivory teeth and a purple-fringed mane. The final touch is to inscribe on the horse's chest: *For their return home, the Achaeans dedicate this thank-offering to Athena.*

I climb the rope ladder hanging through the trap door in its belly. It's high enough inside to stand upright with my arms stretched overhead, smells richly of ship wood and ox-hide, and leather-hinged bunks drop from the walls. The others crowd the foot of the ladder and stare up, awaiting my response.

"Epeius," I say, "you have a god in you."

The others join me and we gaze around. It is dark even with the trap door open. Epeius points out the water jugs up front and the piss pots in the hindquarter. "It's going to be even darker at night," he warns. "You'll have to rely on your ears." He strokes the skin stretched drum-taut over the close-set wooden ribs. By way of demonstration, he shuts the trap door, dropping us into utter black but for a pale gleam from the horse's eyes. "Listen." No one moves or speaks but we can hear every word from outside, right down to the shuffling of feet in dirt. "Of course you too will have to be silent."

It soon grows stifling.

"And air?"

"Ah." I hear the grin in his voice. He demonstrates sliding panels high on the horse's back. "Impossible to spot from the ground." He encourages me to climb the ladder up the neck and inspect the eyes, each bigger than my spread hand and made with a lens of the thinnest oyster shell polished nearly translucent. "Remember," says Epeius, "if someone tears a rip in the side and holds a torch close anything metal will glint. Keep your weapons covered. No rings or buckles. And don't look at the light because the wet of your eyes will betray you."

*

Along with Diomedes, Menelaus, and myself, Stheneleus, Thoas, Neoptholemus, Demophon, Anticlus, and Machaon will be in the horse. It seems to me that Epeius should be there too, for he knows the horse better than anyone, but when I suggest it our engineer, usually so composed and eloquent, becomes strangely evasive. Everyone encourages him.

It's his horse, after all, he designed it, and with much cajoling he finally gives in. We practise climbing in and out as quickly and quietly as possible. We spend a night in it, maintaining silence, and aside from Epeius falling ill with stomach trouble it goes well if somewhat rank. We agree that Epeius is right after all and is best utilised overseeing the evacuation with Agamemnon.

The irrepressible Echion immediately puts himself forward as a replacement. "Please, Odysseus." He has curly dark hair, wide-set eyes, and breathes through his mouth. No great thinker and a little impatient, but brave and eager. "Please."

I say all right.

That evening we burn the camp. In a frenzy of destruction we tear everything down, Agamemnon making a great show of setting his chariot ablaze. We heap tents, beds, trunks, boxes, chairs, old clothes onto the flames, we even set fire to the boats that can't be sailed home. With the camp burning and the fire reflecting in the waves, the Achaeans wade out to their ships and climb aboard and begin rowing slowly away in the dark. The ships will anchor beyond the island of Tenedos and wait for a signal, three burning arrows shot by a scout already positioned in the dunes. The honour of torching the horse when we are safely inside the walls will go to Diomedes, our connoisseur of fire.

Now all that remains of our ten-year occupation are the fire and the horse. Three men at each wheel, we roll the horse a safe distance from the flames, which fleck and glint in its jewelled trappings and bronze saddle trim. Already the

Trojan sentries will be watching. Agamemnon and Nestor have lingered to bless and embrace each of us, a solemn occasion, a time to forget the small blisters. I wonder whether these two old men are relieved not to be in the horse, or fear they are missing out.

"Odysseus . . ." Agamemnon and I grip each other by the shoulders. The fire reflects in his narrowed black eyes. He's a veteran and knows better than anyone that this may be our last meeting. It's one of the few times I've known him lost for words.

"Tomorrow," I reassure him. "Troy."

"They're already watching," he warns.

"Good." If this is to be our last meeting, let him say that I went strong and confident.

Agamemnon faces his brother. I have never doubted that Agamemnon helped Menelaus win Helen in the first place; now it is up to the rest of us to get her back. They embrace in silence, there is nothing to be said. The one wants to be proud and the other approval. Finally Agamemnon turns away and walks down the beach and wades out to his ship. An old man in the night. They'll wait in a bay on Tenedos until they spot the three burning arrows. They can be back here in two hours, less if the men pull hard and the tide is with them.

One by one we climb into the belly of the horse. I draw up the rope ladder, lock down the door and drive the peg through the loop. The silence is as complete as the dark, and heavy with the brine of men.

Chapter Seven

AND THEN it begins to rain. The initial scatter of drops patters searchingly over the horse. As the rain intensifies this dark close place grows smaller and a red-ant sweat seeps down my back. Our job now is patience, the toughest of all skills to master; the sword and the bow nothing compared to it. Careful not to shift or speak, we keep our breathing low and listen intently. Too dark to see anyone's face, I can smell fear—acrid and sour—which no amount of orange or eucalyptus can mask.

I crawl onto one of the bunks and stretch out on my back but my stomach feels exposed so I turn onto my side and draw my knees up. I can hear Diomedes occupying himself by kneading his hands, the right working the left and then the left working the right, then shifting about and applying himself to his feet. I've watched him many times and know his ritual, pressing his heels and then the insteps and the toes, probing as if in search of a gem hidden within his own flesh.

Now the rain rackets down over us like a load of pebbles. Absurdly, I look up as if to watch it fall.

For all our efforts at silence our breath shouts anxiety. Only Diomedes, in the bunk directly above mine, is calm and continues to massage himself. An Egyptian told him that if you grow relaxed enough your soul will drift off like wind through a net and that you could ride it wherever you wished. The man claimed to have flown east as far as India and south to the mountain that is the source of the Nile. He taught Diomedes that by kneading the flesh between your thumb and forefinger your headache vanishes, by probing the sole of your foot you can induce sleep, by massaging the earlobes a man's third leg stands tall. The body's tendons function like the block and tackle of a ship: adjust one line and the sail moves and the ship changes course. Perhaps it's the same with the guts, though not even the wisest Egyptian can explain the functions of the worms, tubes, and molluscs comprising a man's viscera. Certainly Machaon and his learned colleagues can't tell me how that ball of meat known as the eye actually sees. And what is light, the absence of dark or is it the other way around? Or does the one vanquish the other like two wrestlers engaged in an eternal bout, light victorious at dawn and dark victorious at dusk?

"Purpose?" Penelope once said when I was questioning everything, from our lives here on the earth to the gods on Olympus. She placed her palm upon my brow as if I was feverish. "We're all here in the middle," she said, forlorn at having to be the bearer of such news, "stuck between the millstones, grinding the seeds of time."

*

Penelope first saw me in the stadium. It was Helen's wish that women of all ranks be permitted as spectators, and as a result each breath of wind bore the scent of rose and lilac and orange, sweetening the air and distracting us. Helen occupied the premier seat, shielded from the sun by a fringed canopy while women fanned her with ostrich plumes. Never for a moment was she absent from our thoughts. Naked and anxious we moved through our warm-up routines, running, stretching, swinging our arms, hopelessly trying to clear our perfume-befuddled minds and focus on the task at hand.

I was about to run the first heat of the sprint. Palamedes had the lane to my right and he made a great performance of waving to the crowd as though he had already won. What a narrow skull he had; his mother must have had the hips of a boy. His beard was meticulously trimmed. We'd all cut our beards short so as not to give an opponent something to grab when it came time to wrestle. The drum was struck once, calling us to the line; the crowd grew quiet, then came the count, the drum struck once, twice, and on the third we were off. Palamedes got a good start, jumping ahead by a stride. Short, a fast start is my one advantage, and without it the long-limbed often overtake me at the finish. But I bore down, I remained relaxed and breathed evenly, and by mid-race we were shoulder-to-shoulder, and I ended up winning by five full strides, as if a breeze had aided no one else but me. Some murmured that I had a god at my back, and the odds-makers ranked me the favourite in the final. Those men who'd ignored me when I'd arrived—an obscure prince from an obscure island, a small man from a small place—now regarded me with fear and anger, and none more than Palamedes, his sneer demanding to know just who this bow-legged runt was.

At noon the day was done. As I departed the stadium Helen nodded her congratulations. Tall and so seemingly self-confident, she sat with her head tipped back, gazing down the length of her nose as if sighting along the shaft of an arrow. Menelaus trotted over and congratulated me, then added, "But I'll beat you in the final, Odysseus." His red hair was curled and his smile wet. He'd won his heat though not as impressively as I had mine. His broad hips and narrow shoulders didn't exactly inspire awe, yet he was a surprisingly strong and coordinated athlete, though above all he was dogged and confident. Besides, big brother Agamemnon was watching, and it didn't take an oracle to predict that Menelaus would die before being defeated. He clapped me on the shoulder and rejoined Palamedes who was glaring with those feral eyes.

The next day two men fell in the first heat of the long run, both from broken ribs. No surprise that these two ran in the lanes flanking Palamedes, who nonetheless placed third behind Diomedes and Menelaus. I barely noticed. I was busy imagining Helen naked, in every possible attitude, oiling herself, stretching, bathing, unpinning her hair, placing her warm hand on my cool chest as we reclined on her couch. I risked a few glances her way but she wasn't watching the games at all; maybe she was bored already, or more interested in sharing scandal with her maids. I ambled about the infield watching the heats, keeping limber, encouraging Ajax, but mostly keeping an eye on Helen.

She'd wreathed her hair in yellow petals, which made her look like a sunflower, taller and brighter than any of the women around her. Occasionally she rediscovered the games, and sat forward studying the athletes as if she actually cared about the technique of a Macedonian discus thrower, *two full turns before release or two-and-a-half?* Then the mood would pass and she'd wilt, slumping dull-eyed and staring at her fingers. Perhaps she'd already chosen her husband on the basis of our gifts. Menelaus had given her a cape the colour of sandstone, fashioned from the mane of an Ethiopian lion, fringed with gold thread and rubies, and held at the neck by a solid gold clasp in the form of a lightning bolt. Palamedes gave her three black pearls the size of olives, Ajax gave her an elephant's tusk as tall as himself. A clown even back then, Diomedes gave her a pomegranate with a smile drawn on it in charcoal.

Throughout all of this Helen's mother, the Spartan queen, Leda, sat hollow-eyed as if her spirit were a thousand miles away, adrift. It was impossible to mistake her for she wore swan feathers on her shoulders, in her hair, down her arms, over her breasts, around her hips. No one dared raise an eyebrow much less laugh at this strange woman. Was she graced, cursed, or simply mad? Swans were everywhere, even in the stadium. All Sparta was an aviary devoted to swans nesting where they pleased, their feathers drifting in the wind, their droppings in the streets everywhere you walked.

All of this began to preoccupy me as much as images of Helen naked. As a result, I stumbled as I was warming up for the run and sprained my ankle. Moments later my heat was called, I limped to the line and finished last. No one noticed, because to everyone's delight Ajax—the boy among the men—won and advanced to the final. Already the darling of the crowd, he now owned the heart of every young girl, and likely many an old man.

Naturally he was ecstatic. He couldn't contain his happy chatter as he packed my ankle in herbs and I drank from the jug of poppy water on hand for injuries. I saw little profit in damping his joy. We'd become friends, finding an affinity in his being too young and I being too short. I worked with him on his archery and his javelin throw, while he showed me the insects he'd collected on the trip down from Salamis: moths, dragonflies, and all manner of wasp and bee. He talked mostly about his father, Telamon, who would admire and love him if he brought home Helen. "In the first battle of Troy he breached the wall ahead of everyone, even Herakles," said Ajax, as if reciting from the official history. "For this he won Hesione, Laomedon's daughter. The only way I can match that is by winning Helen."

The drug rising like a warm bath around me, I suggested that he had his work cut out for him.

He looked at me with the self-righteous solemnity of youth and ignorance. "Our children would walk unscathed through fire," he said, as if quoting.

I smiled and gave him the thumbs up.

My own father, Laertes, would say walk around the fire, or dump a bucket of water on it. He'd known Telamon, recalling him as a great warrior but also a bit of a bore, lacking wit or humour or even irony, defects far outweighing the martial virtues. My father's contribution to that battle had been to rout the Trojan cavalry by pouring oil over pigs, setting them ablaze then driving them at the horses, a spectacle I'd like to have seen. He'd strongly advised me to avoid the entire Helen business. "You're too young to listen to me," he'd said, "but all this nobility nonsense, all this glory and war, it's bollocks. Stay home, drink wine, swim in the sea. There are plenty of girls right here. Believe me, Spartans are insane. Noble, maybe. I'll give them that. But insane. Don't get mixed up with them." He shook his head and laughed at a people who, he was convinced, were the butt of some god's joke.

I lay on my pallet for the remainder of the day watching the shadows dial themselves across the tent and then dive into dusk. The tent smelled of camphor and incense against the stench of hot bodies. Only at evening, when the wind kicked up, did the air clear, but by then the mosquitoes were already out. I drew my blanket up over my head.

The next day the bad ankle messed up my footwork and I managed only one decent toss of the discus. Still, it was enough to get me to the final. When I limped out of the stadium I didn't go back to the tents with the others, but hobbled past sleeping dogs and Spartan boys wrestling in the dirt, and headed toward the edge of the city. If my ankle hadn't been so sore I might've just kept on going. The hot wind gusted ash and smoke and swan feathers. This failure business was new to me and my pride hurt as badly as my ankle. The Spartans welcomed pain as an opportunity to prove themselves, a sore tooth to bite down on. A cult of sinew that disdained the word-splitters of Athens. I just wanted the pain to go away.

Orange trees grew near the river, and the bank itself was thick with bulrushes and the inescapable swans. Some hissed and moved away, others paddled out onto the flowing water. Between the orange trees and the bulrushes was an expanse of sun-hardened mud, I limped across it and numbed my foot in the river. Rivers flow with such purpose, as if they have business that can't wait. Eventually some shouting boys arrived and began kicking an inflated pig's bladder. I hobbled back to the dormitory, drank two full beakers of poppy water and waited for oblivion. When it came I dreamed of red cloth drifting in a river, a field of ripe barley undulating in the wind, of wax slipping sweat-like down a candle, and I saw a woman walking along the shore at dawn while the incoming tide filled her footprints. I woke before sunrise and stood outside where, for the first time I could recall, I dreaded the approach of day.

Maybe it was a premonition. I was pathetic in the long jump and the day after worse in the javelin. It was a new experience for me, the rawest and most undeniable rebuke, especially when witnessed by the other athletes, the citizens in the stadium, the women, the children, the slaves, and of course Helen. Though I regained some respect by winning my round in archery, I continued retreating to the river each afternoon, disturbing the swans, and, when no one was about, wading into the water and studying my reflection. So, my eyes said, the world is more complex than you imagined, and other men hunt their desires just as hungrily as you.

The boys arrived and divided into teams to play football, but this time there was a girl with them. She played well and she played hard, as absorbed as a cat on the hunt. The next day I made a point of looking for her in the stadium and there she was, a few seats over from Helen, arms crossed under her small breasts, looking bored. I asked about her. Penelope, Helen's young cousin. It was the day of the qualifying bouts for boxing and I'd have done better to keep my attention on my opponent, a Cretan built like a hog and just as hairy, for he beat me black and blue, and it was miraculous that I came away with my teeth. While he advanced to the finals, my consolation prize was a poultice of salt and mud. I would've hidden myself if I could've found a place, but I was a stranger, I had no house to shut myself up inside, only the tent shared by forty others, so it was back to the river and the solace of the cool water and sun-heated rocks. I hoped to see Penelope though was ashamed at how I'd performed and even more at how I looked. One glimpse of my reflection in the river made me want to put a sack over my head: blackened eyes, swollen lips and ear, blood-clotted nostrils. When she appeared with the boys she spotted me right away, the stranger, the bad athlete, the lousy boxer. She gave me a rueful smile that said she knew what I was feeling. This was reassuring, this was a relief, and I began to realize what would have been obvious to an older and wiser man—my father, for instance—which was that however these games turned out my existence, such as it was, would limp on.

Penelope was so clean and lithe I would've licked the sweat off her skin. At one point she grew bored with the game and simply waded into the water and let the current carry her off, laughing at the boys who called her back to the match. She swam well and she swam strong. She turned on her back and stroked elegantly, first one arm raised as if to admire her fingertips, and then the other, content to be carried along around a bend past a floating island of swans. I too wanted her to come back. I imagined the river escorting her to the sea and out over the waves, a strange and beautiful creature that sailors might glimpse and call a mermaid and sing stories about. She would reach some island, Crete perhaps, where she would see cities and temples, and be welcomed by a young king, and this man would find himself thinking of her day and night, and so would keep her for himself and give her gifts and sweet words until she fell in love with him. I found myself gazing downriver anxious for her return, fearful that something had happened, that she was gone from my life already. And then there she was, casually strolling up the beach, letting the sun dry her, not looking at me, but aware of me watching and, I was hoping, not at all displeased by the attention.

I returned to the dormitory with my face aching not from the beating but from smiling. Eager to heap the salt of scorn onto me, the others frowned in curiosity for they saw that I was indifferent.

"Odysseus has had his brains loosened!"

"He's got birds and stars in his skull!"

One made as if to rap my head. "Odysseus! Hello! Anyone in there?"

I would've winked if my eyes weren't swollen nearly

shut, so contented myself with a low bow and a jaunty twirl of the hand. Not one among them suspected that I was in love.

The state of my face frightened young Ajax. He approached me warily, as if to stand too close might injure me further.

"Odysseus . . ."

I grinned and clapped him on the shoulder and reassured him that I was fine.

"You were beaten."

I leaned toward him. "Ajax. Believe me. I have won. And let me tell you something else: you don't want Helen."

He reared back as if I'd spat on him.

I tried to explain, for I wanted him to comprehend the folly of pursuing such a creature. "Theseus couldn't cope with her. How will you? Think of it," I urged him. "You're too young. Free yourself. Give up. Quit."

He stared, bewildered. No concept was lower, no act more demeaning. "Quit? Why?"

"Because even if you win you'll lose."

Now he thought that I'd definitely had my brain rattled.

"Leave the boy alone, Odysseus," called Palamedes. "He doesn't need you pouring shit in his ears just because you took a kicking."

Ajax looked from Palamedes to me and frowned and nodded slowly as if realizing this was true, that Odysseus was sly and deceitful and a backstabber who would poison everyone else's victory to sweeten his own loss.

The others echoed the same sentiment, convinced that I only wanted to drag Ajax down.

Of course Palamedes had been busy telling Ajax that he'd never win his father's love if he listened to a malcontent such as Odysseus. I raised my hands palm upward and shrugged. "You're right. My apologies to you all. Odysseus has had his brains knocked. He's confused. He thinks up is down!" I began to canter about the tent. "Oh. Look!" I pointed to the sky. "A dead bird. And there—" Putting my hand to my ear I made as if to listen. "What a lovely song they have. Tweet, tweet."

This earned me a round of laughter, but poor Ajax was lost; why was I suddenly trying to thwart him? Miserable and confused, he joined Palamedes and Menelaus and a few others who were shaking their heads at my idiocy. Only Diomedes stood apart, frowning, bemused, knowing there was more to it.

By this point all talk was of young Ajax. The others feared to compete against him because of the humiliation of losing to one so young. He had moved on in the boxing as well as in the javelin and the long run, and here he was with his first moustache still soft on his lip, his shoulders skinny, his biceps smooth, and knees as knobby as a colt's. Yet how his manner changed with each successive victory, it was as though he grew years in mere days, holding his head higher, standing taller, but most of all his personality was changing, his innocence dissipating like a morning mist leaving only the dry glare of day.

Chapter Eight

A FEW MORNINGS LATER I was seated at the bench spooning up my gruel when a Spartan page leaned over my right shoulder and whispered that King Tyndareus wanted to talk to me. Palamedes, slit-eyed with suspicion, watched me depart. I followed the page out of the compound and through the city. For all their playing at the rustic life, the Spartan elite maintain fine houses. The approach led through an avenue lined on either side with potted orange trees, stone gods, and imperious swans. We entered a grassy courtyard equipped with dumbbells and archery targets.

Tyndareus was practising with the trident, overarm thrust, kneeling thrust, two-handed jab. He was sinewy, with the rugged complexion of a good Spartan who did his callisthenics each day and made it a principle to wear the coarsest cotton lest too much comfort make a Persian of him. His unplucked eyebrows met in a dark hedge above his nose giving him a crude demeanour. In fact he was refined, his hobbies including breeding cats and cultivating flowers.

"Odysseus!" He seemed more than happy to drop the trident. He sat down on a bench by a jug of wine and invited me to join him. He smelled of mint oil and his left forearm bore a row of three evenly-spaced puncture scars. An accident with a gardening tool or evidence that he'd put in his time on the front line? The talk began innocently enough. We spoke of Ithaka and my journey here, he remarking that in his youth he'd lived in Aetolia not so very far from my island. When the conversation lapsed he sipped his wine and then remarked, "You've stopped competing." When I argued he corrected me and said that I was merely going through the motions. Noting the state of my face and the beating I'd taken in the ring, he added, "And not very ably by the looks of you."

He was reputed to have been a fine boxer in his own day, and his blunted knuckles proved it. What could I say, I'd been thumped. I certainly wasn't going to make excuses about being diverted by lewd fantasies of Helen, so I shrugged and held his gaze so as not to appear evasive. The only thing Spartans despise more than defeat is evasiveness. Front up like a man. What did he want? To encourage me? Why should this Spartan king care about an Ithakan? What did I have to offer? He shrugged in imitation of me.

"The competition's fierce," I said, perhaps lamely.

He nodded that it was indeed. Then, as if dismissing the whole business, he drew my attention to the flowers growing in tubs of unglazed clay. The petals were a deep and fragrant red and the stems barbed with thorns. "Persian," he said. "*Dulband*, they call them. Because the buds resemble their—" he gestured, meaning their headcloths. "The optimism of flowers," he said, as if it was a topic on which he'd been long brooding. "From out of the earth to a brief brilliance and then—" He pitched his wine dregs to the ground. "—Back to the earth." He shook his head slowly, a little sadly, as if it was all absurd and futile, like the life of a man. "Have you met my wife?"

"No."

"But you've seen the swans."

I admitted that yes, I'd seen the swans along the riverbanks and the fields and in the city and even in the stadium.

"After all these years she still sits up at night on the full moon and waits for him. Rubs herself in oils, arranges her hair, puts on her very best clothes, burns incense. She's old now and he's not interested. He likes them young and athletic—able to put up a fight." He smiled ruefully, for what else could he do? A god had raped his wife. *The* god had raped his wife. "Apparently there was quite a tussle. He lost some feathers. She collected them. Some as long as my arm. As soft as if freshly plucked. She sewed them together with gold thread and wears them. I'm sure you've heard of her swan dance."

I confessed that the story had travelled far, Leda in wings on the full moon . . .

"And I'm sure you've seen her in the stadium," he added.

I nodded.

"For years I wondered, why Leda? What had she done? What had I done? Was it an honour or a punishment? As you so astutely observed, all we have that the gods do not is our mortality. And that's why they're so besotted by the desire to fornicate with us. Leda was a fine-looking woman in her day. But the gods are shape-shifters. No goddess need be anything less than perfection. How could a mortal woman, with her moles and moustache, her rocky teeth and pouty complexion, possibly lure one such as Zeus? One reason: because he'd taste mortality. The urgency that comes from coupling with one destined to die."

What was I supposed to say to this?

He saw that he'd made me feel awkward. Wanting to get back to the more manly world of strategy, he jutted his chin in the direction of the stadium. "How many men are competing?"

I didn't know exactly. "Perhaps forty."

"Princes and kings and first sons."

"She'll make a good marriage," I said, reassuring him.

He looked at me from the side of his eyes, as if to say I was insulting him with such bullshit. "She'll be a curse to any man. It's why Theseus gave her up. The old bull-leaper couldn't wait to get rid of her. Practically shoved her out the door when her brothers came for her. It's why you've stopped competing." He read my eyes. "Yes," he drawled, nodding shrewdly and smiling. "Whoever she marries can say goodbye forever to peace of mind. You know that. In your heart, if not in your head, and I think you're one of the new breed who know the difference. Yes . . ." He seemed to cogitate a moment upon this new breed of which I was, apparently, an example. "But typical of the young you go too far, you invent an idea and think that you can then—" He gestured like a conjurer. ". . . Inhabit your fantasy as if it was as solid as a house. That's your confusion. You have a thousand hearts and a thousand faces." He held up his forefinger. "But you only *need* one. You should only *have* one. All this public and private . . ." He frowned as if at unseemly habits. "A face that fits. This is the key to Sparta's greatness."

Elders. If they're so wise and understanding why do they insist on boiling the flavour out of every experience for those of us who've yet to taste them? I was twenty; he was forty. He must have seen my expression hardening because he changed tack again and asked me about the mood in the dormitory.

Ah, so I was to be an informer. I told him the obvious. "We hate each other. Every night we bicker."

"Of course." He didn't need me to tell him that. A hint of impatience weighed his voice, and I worried he was regretting having called me to him.

Offering him more, I said, "The losers will go away bitter. That bitterness will break us apart." I pointed to an old clay pot seamed with cracks. "Greece will crack. The Trojans, the Persians, anyone with a will to fight will find us fragmented and easy to shatter."

For a moment Tyndareus didn't react to this theory. Fear of scorn rushed through me like a wave of dizziness and I placed my palms on the bench to steady myself. Finally he nodded. "What do you suggest? Cancel the games?"

I spoke slowly, carefully, not sure where I was going, letting the words lead me one by one as if finding a path, step by uncertain step, through a dark wood. "A pledge," I said, eager to impress him. "Before the games end, have each competitor swear an oath to honour the man Helen selects. An oath binding him to support the victor in any crisis. For the good of us all."

Tyndareus was nodding his head in agreement even before I'd finished. He seemed renewed, unburdened. "The Oath to Tyndareus," he said, giving it a title. "Good. Very good. You're a clever young man, Odysseus. Name your reward."

I looked at the *dulbands*, so poised and fragile, yet indomitable, each year reborn again. What was I going to say? Would my head speak or my heart, and if so, which of my heads, which of my hearts? Wasn't Helen the obvious choice? "Introduce me to Penelope."

Tyndareus raised his chin and narrowed his gaze as if to better evaluate me. Then he smiled, though I wonder now if it was in admiration or scorn.

When I returned to the tent the others stared at me like a herd of deer facing a wolf. Only the affable Diomedes seemed at ease, whistling as he trimmed his beard before a polished brass mirror. He ceased his whistling to rinse his razor and inquire whether Tyndareus and I had discussed flowers or daughters.

"Both."

"And did you talk about how to make them bloom?"

"Fertilizer. Lots of fertilizer. Nightly doses."

Diomedes barked a laugh. He shook the water from his razor, leaned toward the mirror and resumed his grooming while the others stared from behind wooden faces.

*

I'd wanted Tyndareus to respect me, so when he'd asked my advice I'd answered truthfully. It was shrewd advice, perhaps even wise, and benefited all Hellas. My reward was Penelope, a prize more than fair. And yet it's that very same advice that took me away from both her and my son and robbed me of ten years. Is this the work of cruel gods, blind fate, or simply chaos?

I recall a summer hailstorm. I was a boy and we were harvesting our oranges. Sudden storms weren't unknown, but this one seemed as if it had been aimed, like a fistful of stones, at our orange trees and nowhere else, for only half a mile away the ground was dry and the sky clear. Our entire crop was destroyed. My father saw it as punishment, but for what? Oracles were consulted and ludicrous responses interpreted in the convulsions of the temple virgins: his offerings had been scanty, his offerings insincere, my father had hunted in groves sacred to the gods. What I saw, even at the age of twelve, was blindly erratic nature, chaotic and uncontrollable, and men desperate for certainty.

There was a man, Petras, a citizen with land and animals and a fine reputation. He went missing on a routine journey to the mainland that should have seen him safely home in thirty days. Five years he was gone, no one knew if he had drowned or been killed or what. His wife remarried to a man called Leontes, old, litigious, notorious for his dishonesty, but he was still vital and they had a beautiful daughter together named Cleo. Petras returned. He had been shipwrecked. When he discovered that his wife had remarried and worse, had another child, he killed Leontes while his wife killed herself, and Petras, that good man, that fine citizen, that victim of Fate, had to forfeit his wealth and go into exile. His entire family, sons and brothers, were forever tainted. Cleo, the daughter born of that second union, became a whore. What wrong step had Petras taken? What god had he failed to honour?

*

My passion for the games now redirected to Penelope, I happily cheered for Ajax. (I'd given up trying to convince him of the folly of competing, though it was less out of love for him than sly joy at the thought of the others losing to an adolescent.) He won the javelin but managed only a draw with Menelaus in boxing. Both had to be carried from the ring. The very next day Menelaus took the discus, thanks to Diomedes falling into a laughing fit as Leda entered in her swan regalia causing him to foul on his best throw. Menelaus knew he'd got lucky there. A good athlete, Menelaus, even if he did look like a bean counter. The hard lessons of a Spartan upbringing, but there it is, men come in as many shapes and sizes as dogs. A harelipped Thracian defeated Ajax in the wrestling. Diomedes won the sprint a half-step ahead of me, he also won the long run, and, typical, finished both races looking as composed as when he started. Truly the most enigmatic man I've ever met. The only event I won was archery, and I did it by aiming for Penelope's heart. I hit it three times.

The games ended and we stood in a row awaiting Helen's decision. I had a last minute panic—or was it desire —that she'd pick me and thwart my courting of Penelope. When she chose Menelaus I wasn't surprised, as throughout the games Agamemnon had sat next to Tyndareus. And yet at the same time I was disappointed that Helen was so easily controlled, that she hadn't asserted herself and, willful and unpredictable as the god who'd supposedly sired her, selected Ajax or Diomedes or someone else.

Diomedes laughed at her decision. Palamedes hid whatever he felt and applauded Menelaus. Poor Ajax was crushed in the way only an adolescent can be, for he'd not yet learned how to shield his heart. He hid his face in shame, then that shame turned into a rage that he directed at me, for he was convinced that I had purposely thwarted him. He accosted me after the closing ceremonies, fists clenched at his sides, tearful, trembling, betrayed.

"You sowed doubt, Odysseus. You poisoned my confidence." His eyes pleaded with me to admit what I'd done, to give him an excuse that he could carry home as evidence to his disappointed father.

"Why would I do that to you?"

But he knew what he knew. "Now I go home in disgrace," he said. "Exactly as my father predicted." What was I to say to that? I felt bad for him, so didn't laugh or walk away, but stayed there and took it on the chin. It wasn't enough.

He vowed that this would stand between us forever. "Some day it must be settled, Odysseus."

I gave up and walked away saddened, but the fact was that I didn't care what he thought, not really. I'd tolerated his spittle-flecked tirade because I had something—someone—more important on my mind than an indignant boy.

Penelope's first words to me were: "You're very bow-legged."

"They say it's a sign of nobility."

"They say you didn't try very hard in the Games."

I said I'd been diverted. I couldn't concentrate.

She became innocent. "Yes, all the swan feathers floating around in the air. You must have thought it was snowing."

"It wasn't the swans that diverted me." And I told her how I'd gone about winning the archery contest.

She put her fingers to her chest and checked for blood. "Good shot."

Chapter Nine

THE RAIN CONTINUES. How I'd like to be outside, feeling the cool drops upon my face, far, far from here. My kneecap is aching again. I massage it, thinking of that Trojan with my javelin through his throat and the watery expression in his eyes, as if he was staring from the depths of a lake. I try not to trouble myself over killing. Death comes sooner or later, and if there are gods or reasons behind why and when and how, they're too subtle or shifting for me. Still, I can't help thinking how that Trojan whose blood seeped over my spear knew moments of wonder, such as the first time he felt the weight of lead in his hand or felt the confusion caused by the presence of a certain girl. Perhaps he preferred pears to apples, wept alone at night with his head under his blanket. It doesn't matter, he's in Hades now, a Shade like Ajax and Achilles and so many others, or maybe there is no Hades, no Shades, and he's just so much dust. Is it possible? Is it all merely men and their imaginings? I don't know which prospect is more frightening, gods or nothing.

Nine years passed before I met Ajax again, here, at Troy. We stood face to face, and, with Agamemnon watching, we locked arms and vowed brotherhood, all very noble, but I could see in his eyes—as he intended I should —that he still believed I'd worked against him in the games, that I'd urged Tyndareus to tell Helen to choose someone other than him. This didn't exactly bode well for the campaign. He'd become a giant, standing a full head higher than me, muscled and angry, his silver wristbands so broad they'd have slid right off my arms. But there was the task at hand of dealing with the Trojans, and for that diversion I was almost thankful. I didn't envy anyone who had to face Ajax on the field. He'd windmill his axe knocking down horses and men alike, not looking to see who was in the way, simply going whirlwind, it was your own business to avoid him. But he didn't leave opponents to suffer, not like Palamedes, who loved those moments when a man's life was bleeding out of him even while his eyes were still wide and he saw what was to come. Palamedes would cut a man's ears off and throw them to the ravens then sit the poor bastard up, hold him in his arms and direct his gaze so that he could see the birds fight over them, the very same ears with which he'd heard his mother's voice.

*

The snort and blow of horses stirs us from our broodings. Voices erupt as if the entire population of Troy suddenly surrounds us. Torchlight gleams through the horse's pearl-shell eyes and a spear raps the ribwork, all strangely intimate and upsetting. I find myself curling up tighter on my bunk, trying to be as small as possible. With the ebbing of the rain the mutter of voices becomes clearer.

"Burn it."

"Bring axes."

Priam, dry-voiced and hard, says wait. In my mind's eye I see the Trojans leaning their heads together in conference. No doubt the old king is thinking hard, and no doubt he's missing Hector's counsel more than ever, but it's a woman's voice we hear next, Cassandra, Priam's daughter.

"It's a trick. The Achaeans are up to something."

Priam answers with silence, a silence that smells tangibly of scorn. After all—so the story goes—Cassandra betrayed Apollo's gift of prophecy; how can she be trusted? Surely Apollo would have rescinded or corrupted this gift. Either way, she was condemned to be distrusted, her warning as futile as seed sewn on ash. She begins to argue, insisting that the only safe course of action is to burn it.

Priam calmly observes that the time has not yet come when he takes her advice in matters military, and then he orders her back into the city.

I've seen Priam often over the past decade and observed how he has aged. He's grown gaunt and bent, his shoulders brittle, his neck vulnerable, his jaw trembling, even his skull seems to have withered. As for his voice it is hard and dry and you want to give him a drink of water. He is too old for this. Instead of siege warfare he should have been enjoying his final days tending his vines, making faces at his grandchildren, and devoting his evenings to ambling along the riverside taking the cool air and reminiscing. But Hector's death broke him. His posture has become curved as a wet reed as he sits his horse. Priam, once so tall and square-shouldered with a spine like a spear. I'll always honour Achilles for having returned Hector's corpse to the old man so that he could bury him with proper ceremony. No father should outlive his son.

As Cassandra departs there is a fresh stirring among the Trojans, the slap of livery, new voices. Helen. Her delighted laughter, so perpetually amused by the workings of men. Even after all these years her laughter is unmistakable. Valuing her opinion more than that of Cassandra, Priam wastes no time in asking what she thinks.

"What I think, Lord? Perhaps the horse speaks? Let us ask it." And in a louder voice, "Tell us, horse. The Achaeans are gone and their camp burns. Are you a gift? Compensation? A trick? Speak to us."

We don't move, we scarcely breathe. I feel Menelaus's strung nerves. His thoughts ring in my own skull. He is closer to Helen than he has been in ten years, the woman he has dreamed of every night for a decade, here she is, he could speak to her without raising his voice. I reach out and find his arm and grip it firmly meaning be strong, Menelaus, be strong.

Diomedes alone knows I visited Helen only last year, the same night he and I rescued the Palladium. When we'd emerged from our hiding place he'd grinned and shaken his head when I told him my scheme, but he didn't try talking me out of it. I'd indulged him in his little side trip into the taverna, now it was my turn. We'd meet at dawn and depart with the farm labourers by the northeast gate.

To be the first Achaean to talk to Helen since she fled Sparta with Paris was a prize I'd long wanted. But there was more, I wanted to be alone with her, to look into her eyes, to see into her soul—or more accurately into my own —and satisfy certain questions I'd scarcely acknowledged even to myself. So I'd slipped away, leaving Diomedes to deal with the Palladium.

She was waiting as if it had all been pre-arranged. Her voice was as sweet as scent. "Come up, Odysseus, come up."

I climbed the wall and stepped between the potted lemon trees and saw the beaded curtain swaying over her doorway. I entered. The room smelled of orange flower and a single oil lamp burned against a brass backing giving me a glimpse of myself: bruised, ragged, filthy. My words would indeed have to be sweet.

She was in a chair in a corner. She indicated the companion seat, arching an eyebrow at my disguise.

"It's been nineteen years," she said. "Though of course I've seen you from the walls. How hot and dusty the whole business is."

The lamp burning between us blanched out her face as if I'd stared too long into the sun.

"Have I aged?" she asked. She sounded genuinely weary.

I leaned to see her better—and recoiled. My shocked reaction made her laugh. Penelope. I blinked and I squinted and looked again. Yes, Penelope, my wife. Gone were the sharp planes, the long jaw, the sharp nose, and instead I saw Penelope's heart-shaped face, the small jaw, the large eyes, the thick black hair, the full lips. But a gust rippled the lamp flame and stirred the beaded curtain. The spell departed, my head cleared. When I looked again she was Helen once more. She sat back, out of the light, and laughed deep in her throat, amused by her trick.

"Are you here to rescue me or to kidnap me?" she asked, her voice suddenly arid. "Or," she added, insinuatingly, "to seduce me?"

I tensed. I couldn't honestly say.

"Ah," she said knowingly, and chuckled. She stretched out her legs and let her hands dangle over the ends of the chair's arms. Those hands, each finger reposed like the tail of a cat. We were silent. There was only the clicking of the bead curtain in the uneasy breeze and the hiss of the wick in the oil. Now her fingers took on a new aspect, and I thought of weed in a stream. "How is Menelaus?" she asked suddenly, as if referring to a mildly entertaining acquaintance from long ago, someone we'd both found faintly absurd. Her right hand turned over with the question, palm upward, fingers spread. In that palm I saw a valley creased with roads, a land that had known battles, and I saw an oasis in the starlight, with a pool and fig trees and a tent and a bed and on the bed Helen, young and eager . . .

I put my hand to my brow and shook the images from my mind. Menelaus? I didn't want to talk about Menelaus. I put my hand on her knee; she covered it with her own, warmly, suggestively, as if she'd been awaiting me all this time.

"You know," she said, "I was very disappointed that you didn't bring me a gift all those years ago. Every other man did, but not Odysseus." She stroked the back of my hand with her forefinger. "Was the sly Odysseus the shy Odysseus? Or merely ill-mannered? And then you gave up so easily."

Here was the question that had been lodged all these years like a bit of grit under my eyelid: had I been wise in opting for Penelope, or had it been due to fear, because I knew I couldn't win, because I knew that I wouldn't be up to the mark?

Not knowing what to say, I asked her if she was content.

"Content?" She repeated the word as if bemused by the concept, as if it was a strange obsession of an absurd people. "I don't know." She looked around the room crowded with lamplight and shadows. "I've learned that there are more shades of grey than there are of black or white. I've learned that grey is an endless colour." She raised her hand and made a slicing motion. "You can divide it like an infinite apple." I watched her long hand with those precise fingers. "And you, Odysseus. Do you have regrets?" How genuinely empathetic she sounded, her with one foot on Olympus and one in Troy.

I didn't hesitate. "Yes."

This saddened her. Though to my disappointment and perhaps relief she didn't ask what exactly it was that I regretted. Perhaps it was only the strange fruit of a relentless imagination and didn't bear discussion. She inclined her head to one side and smiled ruefully. "I was hard on poor Penelope. I've been hard on a lot of people I love. Sometimes, at night," she said, "I miss all those swans."

Later, when I finally emerged from Helen's room, I found Diomedes waiting just outside. He'd followed me. He had a strange look in his eye and a brick in his hand, weighing it up and down as if gauging its potential for damage. "I thought it was Ares you wanted to kill," I said, taking him by the elbow and escorting him away. He leaned to sniff me and said I smelled of orange blossom.

Chapter Ten

AND NOW there is a fresh stir. A new arrival. Sinon. We press our ears to the walls, but it doesn't take much to imagine Trojan sentries, one at each arm, escorting him through the crowd. Now Sinon's acting will truly be tested.

I know many of the voices from our futile parlays over the years. Sinon is deft in his responses, he puts on a convincing show of fear and sincerity as he explains how the oracles decreed that only blood sacrifice would buy us a fair wind home, and that he, Sinon, was chosen by vindictive Odysseus to bleed at the altar.

"Odysseus!" Priam mulls my name as if it can only mean trouble. "The worst and the best of the Achaeans."

In the bunk above me, Diomedes snickers.

Other voices join the questioning, foremost among them Laocoon, their seer, a blind and suspicious old man.

"How did you escape?"

"I ran."

"You ran."

"Yes."

"As simple as that? You ran."

"Yes, sir."

Someone remarks that the Achaean is wounded. When Laocoon hears this he's all the more convinced that it's a ruse. He becomes shrill. "Wounded? And a thousand Achaeans couldn't catch you?"

"I slipped away before they came for me. I knew I was the choice."

"You knew you were the choice. How?"

"The oracle. And because Odysseus hates me."

"He hates you. Why does he hate you? Stop lying. Explain yourself!"

"I refused to love him."

Priam is less interested in this than in the meaning of the horse.

"To assuage Athena," explains Sinon. "For the crime committed by Odysseus in stealing the Palladium."

A murmur runs through the crowd. Priam muses upon this. "He thought that by stealing the heart of Troy her blood would cease pumping and she would lie down and die."

"Everyone was against it," says Sinon. "But Odysseus, he convinced them. Menelaus and Agamemnon said stealing the Palladium would only make the Trojans fight harder."

"Odysseus, Odysseus!" sneers Laocoon. "I have a harder question for this spy. You, boy, why not simply return the Palladium, eh?"

"It's gone. To Mycenae."

"Why is the horse so large?" asks Priam.

It's a thought I hadn't anticipated, assuming that to the Trojans hugeness was an unquestioned virtue. Perhaps herein lies Priam's wisdom, for he isn't beyond voicing the simple question. Now is Sinon's moment, he has to come through. *The greatness of Troy merits a gift of equal greatness? The biggest city demands the biggest horse?*

"Oh noble Lord Priam," says Sinon. "The horse is large so that it won't fit inside the walls of Troy and serve as your guardian and strength. This way it placates Athena while thwarting the Trojans."

Perfect, and yet even as he delivers it I'm already worrying that Sinon will steal some of my thunder and be sung of as the man who, when the horse was at risk of being burned, when the Achaeans were on the verge of dying, when the entire ten-year campaign was about to be lost, rescued us with his wits and defeated the Trojans. The response is not merely clever, it also plants the idea of bringing the horse inside the gates in Priam's mind. How could Priam not believe Sinon? He declares that the young man is now a Trojan. A cheer goes up. The horse is a gift. The war is over.

Laocoon isn't so enthused, he insists that the Achaeans are plotting, his voice growing more shrill, more brittle, as his influence wanes.

Now Paris speaks up on his father's behalf. "They've lost Achilles and Ajax. They've burned their own camp. They're ships have sailed. They're gone. It's over."

This is too much. "Oh yes, that's good coming from you who brought all this on. She tricked you and now they're at it again."

"If you had eyes you might not think so," sneers Paris.

"At least let us slaughter a bull and read the signs," Laocoon pleads.

Priam agrees.

During all of this we hear a vast clamour of a gathering army. I have no doubt that thousands of Trojans, the entire city, is rushing to see the fantastic horse. Some stand directly under us, so close that we hear their whispering and feel their heat and urgency. They rap the horse's legs, touch and stroke them as if for a blessing. Soon we hear the bellowing of a bull. I climb the ladder up the horse's neck to its eyes.

Hundreds of torches sway like a grass fire in a wind, and there is the bull, a rope at each leg and each horn. Black-robed Laocoon is led to the bull and presented a sword. He grips it in both hands and raises it high as the bull continues to bellow and the torch light slides over its glistening hide. Laocoon swings. Brings down the blade. The bull's neck splits wet and red and spurting; the severed tendons let its great head slump. The butchers work fast, rolling the carcass onto its side and slitting the belly, releasing a slithering mass of steaming intestines. Accompanied by his sons, proteges in the arts of divining, Laocoon kneels in the blood. The onlookers press in as closely as they dare, torches an encircling wall of flame-topped palings. Sweat runs stinging into my eyes so that I have to squint, it is all a blur, a mass of swimming figures. Laocoon listens to his sons. They help him to his feet and turn him to face Priam, who sits his horse with tall dignity.

"The horse is full of snakes," declares Laocoon. "Burn it."

*

It is our good fortune that Priam does not always take the advice of his seers.

The horse begins to move, the oak wheels crying out despite having been pig-greased at the axle. Everyone, even the lame, rush to help, pushing or else taking a place at ropes that have been lashed to the legs. In this way we approach the city. We cling to the straps that Epeius is clever enough to have fastened to the the sides, for we are flung about as the horse dips and pitches over the terrain. I keep to the ladder and peer out the horse's eyes. The Trojans chant and dance—not the stately turns performed at the equinox—but frenzied leaps, the chant and stomp of a horse cult. Some even throw themselves under the wheels seeking some imagined glory in such a death, their exultant groans accompanying the terrifying crack of their ribs. A madness has come over them, they are possessed. We are Zeus Earth Shaker come to walk among mortals.

We advance across the marshalling ground toward the gates. The horse sways as wildly as the Trojans dance and I brace myself in the confines of the neck. It's as if I'm trapped inside the mast of a ship caught in a gale. We lurch and wobble and bounce. I've always been good at sea, but trapped in here even I begin to feel ill, for there is no horizon to look at and steady my stomach. I shut my eyes and hang on as we find each ditch and rock, every pothole and root. I'm sweating and trembling when we finally reach the stone ramp that leads to the doors where the wheels suddenly turn smoothly. We halt. Silence. There is a massive creaking as the gates of Troy crank open. Again we advance but after a few seconds we halt once more, there is discussion, the horse is too tall, the stone arch that spans the gates must be broken.

A hand grips my ankle.

"Odysseus?"

Menelaus squints up at me. In the clamour and din there's hardly need for us to keep silent any longer, we could beat drums and not be heard. I describe what I see, the people, the dogs, the waving torches, all blurred by the oyster shell. Then I see something directly in front of me, just a few feet away, on the arch above the gate: a crouching boy staring into the horse's eyes. I stare back. Then recall Epeius's warning about the reflection of our eyes and shut mine.

The next thing I hear is the bash of hammers on stone. They're breaking the arch. The stone crumbles then crashes to the flag-paved ramp. More cheers, followed by a thumping from above. I wince, then understand. Boys are leaping onto the horse to ride it into the city while women throw flowers. Again we begin to move. Once we are inside, the gates crank shut behind us. It takes an hour to haul the horse up the winding streets to the acropolis and onto the temple floor where the Palladium had stood. It is well after midnight, no victorious army enjoys a greater welcome, and for hours afterwards the people whirl and pray and drink and weep and stroke the horse. The drunker they get the louder they get. They slaughter sheep and make sacrifice. They dance and fight and sing and build fires. They cook food and they feast and I suspect that many a child will be conceived on this night of nights. I also begin to fear that they'll never go away, that the horse will never be left alone, that guardians will be posted, priests appointed, and we'll be trapped inside for days, forced in the end to make some doomed and desperate lunge. I climb down from the eyes and lie on my bunk, knees to my chest. We all try to be patient, to be calm, and not give in to twitches or whimpers. It is the longest night any of us has ever known and anxiety drives us to the chamber pots so that the stench soon grows unbearable. I mark the passage of time by counting the beats of my heart. Diomedes is the only one who retains a sense of humour, and begins whistling faintly some marketplace jig. I press my hands to my face to stifle a spasm of laughter that degenerates into a retch. And then we hear the crow of roosters. Dawn. Light filters in through the horse's eyes, the sun rises, it grows hot inside. There is a resurgence of activity around us and with it the prospect of what lies before us, an entire day in the horse, perhaps many days. This breeds panic, a panic that will lead to some desperate move. Echion is off his bunk and pacing. I catch him by the shoulders and force him to sit. A whispered argument erupts, someone—Thoas, Demophon—mutters that they've had it, they're going to open the door. There is a struggle, a brawling of mute bodies blindly wrestling, then silence but for panting. We regain self-control and without a word crawl back to our bunks.

The air has become unbreathable, as humid as a steam box. Only very slowly do we sit up, realizing how quiet it is outside. I climb back up to the eyes. The Trojans are leaving, drifting away in twos and threes, or passed out, done in by drink and exhaustion. Many sing and embrace as they stagger off. What a day for Troy. The Achaeans have departed and a god has replaced them.

*

I draw the pin and lift the flap-hinge and pull up the door. Air. It smells of cool stone and crushed flowers. We kneel at the trap door like parched beasts at a pond. Directly below us lie drunk Trojans, men, women, clothes torn, mouths wide, most snoring, some bleeding.

Young Echion is so desperate to be first out that he begins climbing down before I've dropped the ladder. He loses his grip. I grab for his hand but he falls, fingers flailing upward, and lands on his back, the strike of skull on stone sickening to hear. Even as we watch, blood seeps out around his head. His wide eyes stare up at us. Paralysed by such an omen, we look on in horror, until I break the spell and climb down.

"Echion . . ." I kneel by him but he's dead. Letting him of all people in the horse was irresponsible, I should have known better. First Dercynus, then Ajax, now Echion; all three of them looked to me.

"Leave him," says Diomedes softly. He grips my elbow and urges me up. There is no time for memorials.

I gaze around narrow-eyed and frowning as if sizing up the situation, but in truth I am tightening my brow as much to hold back a cry of remorse as to gauge how to proceed. There are scores of bodies and the dogs prowl and sniff. Then a shout from a woman. She drops her water jug and runs shrieking. Diomedes strikes a spark to a torch and throws it spear-wise through the trap door, and within minutes the horse smokes and glows, the seams between the planks incandescent stripes. With the burning horse as a diversion, Diomedes and the others will run back down to open the gates while I guide Menelaus to Helen. Agamemnon, meanwhile, should already have our ships at the beach.

I lead the way out of the temple past villas of sandstone and cedar. Outside Helen's palace we hide between junipers and tubbed lemon trees. Now come the first shouts of fire. Off above the palace roof flames snap like shredded pennants, guards run. I climb the wall and Menelaus follows and bumps a potted fig which hits the marble in a burst of dirt. A guard sees us, Menelaus flings soil into the man's face, and while he wipes his eyes chops him across the neck leaving him sprawled in a slick of blood. The flames from the horse strain as if fighting to free themselves and take flight. All at once the entire city is shouting: voices, bells, dogs, birds. We collide with two children, a boy and a girl, rushing to see the fire. They stagger back then call out, the boy an imperious little bugger, demanding the guard, stamping his foot, not frightened but impatient, indignant, as if he is surrounded by incompetence. At that moment Helen splits the beaded curtain. She hesitates. She glances around uncertainly. Flee? Call a guard? To which side does she commit herself? Or is it merely the swaying of the beaded strings that makes her seem to vacillate? But her decision is made—the Achaeans have done it, the walls are broken, she throws herself into Menelaus's embrace.

"Mother." The boy bears a look of appalled disapproval. His resemblance to Paris is plain, the long jaw and narrow nose, the skull flat at the back, but he has Helen's brow and pale blue eyes, all planes and hard lines. Helen lets go of Menelaus and gathers both children into her arms. All three look fearfully at the strange man who has come to claim her. Now the question is what will Menelaus do? Of course he should have expected as much, ten years with Paris, children were inevitable. This made three, Hermione via Menelaus, and these two. And three husbands, Theseus, Menelaus, and Paris. A woman of some small experience.

She's grown heavier about the throat and there are creases branching from the corners of her eyes. The Trojan winters have not agreed with her, the great land to the east has taken its toll. She may be the offspring of a god but she is apparently not immune to time. Now comes the test of Menelaus's love; now comes his fiercest battle, one greater than any he'd faced on the field where victory and honour depended so directly, so simply, upon an arm and a sword. He embraces her, catches her up in his arms and spins her around and she laughs, head back, delighted, as if she too has pined for this moment, and maybe she has. Then he kneels and embraces the children. Confused but obedient, they submit in silence. I've never had great respect for Menelaus's brain, I've always regarded him as a pawn moved here and there by his big brother Agamemnon, but if he suspects Helen's loyalty he's also wise enough not to spoil their reunion, and shrewd enough not to ruin his introduction to these children to whom he will be a guardian if not a father.

During all of this I realize that I should have stabbed him, done him in while I had the chance, before he and Helen saw each other. My hand travels of its own will to my dagger. It's a good dagger, long, with a wedge-shaped blade that opens a wound that won't close. It would've been so easy to stab him, just draw the knife and plunge, it's all there in my mind's eye: dispatch Menelaus then find Helen, greet her warmly, take her by the hand, assure her that I'll guide her to Menelaus. We'd have walked together through the palace, reminiscing, maybe even sharing a laugh, then she'd halt at the sight of his corpse. I too would put on a show of shock. At that moment she'd understand everything, at that moment she'd understand she'd lost the one man who would keep her safe from the vengeance of all the Achaeans who, quite rightly, hated her for having robbed them of ten years of their lives, even better, her fall would be Penelope's revenge . . .

But it doesn't happen, it is too late, the story plays out differently.

Menelaus and Helen stand apart the better to admire each other. They grin irrepressibly and I watch Helen's eyes but can't say what she truly feels, what she hides and what she shows. As for Menelaus he looks twenty years younger,

155

he is once again the young athlete who has just won the prize. He turns and grips my hand and my elbow in teary gratitude.

"Odysseus. Friend." His voice chokes and his eyes swim.

Friend? We've been many things to each other over the years, but friends? I return the pressure and smile warmly. "Menelaus," I say, as if his victory is my own, something he actually appears to believe. "At last."

"At last," he echoes.

I understand something that I should have grasped before: that Menelaus knew what he wanted and pursued it for ten years regardless of the reputation it earned him. Worse, I have blamed him when it is I who have been the coward. I gave up my family for his goal. If I was stronger I would have stayed home, said no, go to Troy without me, the world can say what it wants, but at the time the wise Odysseus believed that you can't sacrifice reputation and retain dignity unless you are a sage or a fool. And yet here stands Menelaus with his prize, happy.

Helen looks on radiant and imperial, the queen proud of her menfolk. Maybe it's true. More likely she's already planning ahead for the life that awaits, planning ahead and turning her heart. Even the children are convinced that something grand and god-sanctioned is taking place and so they too smile, though tentatively, uncertainly, and I anticipate trouble when they grasp what is actually in store for them, when they realize they'll never see their real father again, certainly not alive.

A new bout of shouting erupts nearby. Sandalled feet slap past on the portico. Helen takes the children by the wrists and leads us through another room and out the back to a barred gate. Menelaus slides the beam aside and edges the gate open. Clear. We step into a narrow footpath. Down to the left people pound past in the main avenue. "I know a route," Helen says. They start off but after a dozen steps halt and look back enquiringly at me.

"Go on," I say.

"Forget it," says Menelaus. "I'll give you gold. Anything. Name it."

How easy it is to be generous when you've got your prize in hand. Agamemnon also owes me a reward. What a rich man I'm going to be. My wife may have remarried, my son may have forgotten me, Ajax and Dercynus and Echion are dead, but apparently I've earned a reward, a Trojan chariot perhaps, a concubine who will always secretly hate me, another set of gleaming armour, a few trinkets from Priam's hoard, a sack of gold. Oh yes, and a reputation, a song, perhaps. Will it be difficult to find words that rhyme with Odysseus? I don't know what to say to Menelaus, so I do what I've always done best, I lie. I grin and tell him that I want one last tour of Troy, to see the sights before we depart. I even manage a stylish toss of the hand.

It takes Menelaus a moment but then he smiles. Of course, Odysseus wants a few anecdotes, for he rates no prize higher than a good story.

"Take care, Odysseus," says Helen, pronouncing my name slowly, as if it is foreign, as if we are strangers. We exchange no meaningful look, no significant glance, nothing to mark our having known each other.

When they're gone at last, I step back inside the palace and wander into Helen's bedchamber and stand there hating the sunlight that pours into the room. Gold motes roll in the shafting sun. I pass my hand through them as if to gather them up but they flee like fish while shrieks reach me muted and remote. Helen's churned bedcovers resemble swirling water, and I'm tempted to plunge in and drown. Had Tyndareus urged her to choose me? Had she defied him? Or had he told her that I'd already fallen in love with Penelope? It doesn't matter, it never mattered. My woman is home facing another day. By now there are suitors circling her, and even if Cloud Splitter himself comes down and offers me immortality and a place on Olympus I'll say no—I know that now—for I'd rather go home to Penelope and Telemachus, to the scent of fresh wood shavings in the carpenter shop, to our olive wood bed.

Calmer, I begin a leisurely perusal of Helen's room, picking up items from the tables and shelves, perfume vials, pumice stones, polished brass mirrors framed in shell-work, and all manner of rings and brooches and necklaces of strung pearls. On a stand made of antlers I find a gold ring inlaid with a silver horse that resembles the wooden one now burning in the temple. Did Helen send the idea to me in a Dream? I try the ring on all my fingers but it fits none, so I slip it into an inner pocket. The blanched stench of smoke returns me to the world. I hear pig squeals and dog barks and, bizarrely, laughter, joyous whoops of glee. Passing through the adjoining room, I step onto the portico where the guard Menelaus stabbed lies in a dried lake of blood. Dragonflies with brilliant blue bodies and two sets of wings are bogged in it. I squat for a closer look. They feed richly. Playing the god, I lift one up to free it but its wings are clotted and gummed. I pry off the dead Trojan's helmet, it's made of leather and horn and plumed with cock feathers. I also take his shield. The helmet smells rank but like the racket and the chaos it is distant, everything is distant, as though I'm watching it all from a far hill, never have I felt more aloof and alone. Looking at the sky I see that it is going to be a fine day, bright and hot, but I also see fallen oak leaves brittle on the portico, potted poppies which have burst their pods, and mint that has gone to seed. The cicadas and pine borers continue grinding away with the blind industry of insects even though summer is nearly over.

I drift around to the front of the house. Our wooden horse has burned down but other fires send up smoke and the sun shapes and contours the rolling clouds. A guard bursts at a run from the house carrying a spear in each fist; he ignores me and I him. The avenue is strewn with crockery and baskets and tipped carts. A wicker cage full of frantically flapping birds gains speed as it rolls down the hill. They cheep piteously, and without thinking I trot after them and catch the cage and hold it up. Their wings beat the air and the bars, I flip the catch and shake them free. They pour out, skimming low over the ground before veering up, a ribbon of birds assembling like a single creature into the air. The entire city smoulders, stone and brick go black and bitter, and grey fumes smart my eyes. Ur, Khajuraho, and now Troy; they rise like waves and crash on the sand and Poseidon, old kelp-beard, old fish god, yawns in his palace of coral while, high above, Zeus on his throne crosses his knees and smoothes his robe and scarcely takes any notice.

The Achaeans advance in a wave. I reach the top of the wall where Trojan bowmen shoot straight down while our archers return fire, arrows flicking past and dropping like sticks. I stroll along only mildly interested. The land slopes away to the shore where men continue streaming from our beached ships. No, the song spinners will not be kind to Priam, the king who lost the mighty city of Troy.

Ahead of me a familiar figure perches on the wall. I halt, a fist clenches in my gut, Ajax, blond hair luffing on the wind, breastplate glimmering, sword across his lap as though he might strum it like a zither. All about him hum bees. I wipe my hands over my face. Surely the smoke has addled me, but there he is, Ajax, and there they are, a swarm of honey bees, large fat ones that walk on his shoulders and his hands, rising and resettling, crawling over his armour, up his neck, across his cheek, as absorbed in their work as if Ajax is a source of nectar. At ease with this, he pays them the be-mused attention one might give a young cat. I approach slowly. When I come abreast of him he tilts his head at an appraising angle to gauge me. Bees sit on his forehead, his ears, in his hair, one lights upon his very eye and he does not even blink, after a few moments it flies off.

"Odysseus," he says. His voice is no longer that of an embittered enemy or of a boy who has been rejected, but that of a traveller returned after many years in distant deserts. He notes my headgear. "So, you're a Trojan now?" he asks ironically, as though he'd not be surprised if I'd betrayed everyone at the very last moment.

I'll not quip with the dead. "The horse succeeded."

He smiles. "Small talk comes from small bones." He'll not deign to argue with the living. He raises his hand covered in a living glove of bees and turns it admiringly this way and that. He carries them close to his ear and listens, eyes closed, as though to music, to whispering voices, and seems pleased with what he hears. After a time he lowers his hand and looks out at the smoldering city. Black smoke rolls off the shops and houses. He regards it all as if reading the weather, as if admiring the very shape of the smoke itself, and then he turns the other way and gazes out over the plain toward the sea. I study him, as real as a dream. I note that he is not wearing Achilles's armour. Is he snubbing my gesture, was it too little too late? If I had the chance to do it over again would I have let him win, would it have been worth his good will? Perhaps. Either way it is one more regret to add to my ever-mounting heap. I'm close enough that I hear the hum of the bees. Some circle me but do not light, apparently I am not sweet enough. I reach to catch one but it passes through my palm with only the faintest sensation. I study my hand, frowning. Ajax turns from the view of the plain and looks at me; is that sadness or indifference in his eyes?

"What of the gods?" I ask him.

"The gods?" The concept seems remote to him. "The gods do not visit Hades."

"But Hades himself? And Persephone?"

He suppresses a smile. "Hades . . ." he says, as if he could tell me stories of the skull king and his spectral queen. At last he has both more knowledge and experience than I do, he has visited eternity.

"What do you think I can give you, Ajax, now of all times?"

"There is nothing you can give me and nothing I can have."

So the dead can lie. "You want songs."

Now he does smile. "Are you offering to sing? Come, Odysseus, sing me a song."

Looking into the eyes of the dead is like gazing at a winter sun in the hope of warmth.

As if reading my thoughts, Ajax turns his face upward and stares unblinking at the sun. He gazes at it without discomfort, as if it is but a distant candle. "You will be remembered only by dogs," he says at last, as if only now recalling the reason for his visit. Then he stands. "But we will talk again soon enough." The bees, as if trained, rise in a swarm and hover and then disperse, and with that Ajax is also gone.

I begin to run slowly along the wall, convinced that I must be dreaming, that I am like the mad who talk to the air. Indifferent to arrows and corpses and to the Achaeans now mounting their ladders, I keep on running. At a turn I find two Trojans backing a Greek against a tower. I draw my knife and advance. Seeing my helmet they let me get close and I stab the first under the ribs and the second through the throat. It is only when the second lolls dead against me that I recognize him: Sinon. Catching him as he slides to his knees I lay him gently on the stone. He does not open his eyes, he's gone already. I turn to the Greek and see that it is Palamedes. I remove my helmet.

"Odysseus." For once the sneer has left his face. His eyes are wide and innocent; a momentary lapse of suspicion.

I reach out my hand and he takes it, then I jerk him toward me and slash him across the throat. A hot spurt of blood sprays my neck then spouts again with the beat of his heart, though weaker this time. The familiar hate flares in his eyes and he almost smiles, as if even now, with his neck slit, his blood gloving my fist, he knows something I do not, that he has one more move to make, but if he does he's unable to execute it, for with my other fist I grip his hair and twist his head and whisper into his ear, "How does it feel, old friend? Tell me, how does it feel? No? Nothing to say? Well, I have: it's been worth the wait." I smile into his eyes, and with that he sinks through my arms like so much sand.

Somewhere someone shouts, Murder! Murder! I almost laugh. Murder, in a war? I walk down the steps toward the gate shaking my head at such madness, then I halt and reach into that pocket and find Helen's ring. I climb back up the steps to where Palamedes and Sinon lie in blood that already grows dull in the heat. The fighting has moved off and we are alone. Opening Sinon's mouth, I place Helen's ring under his tongue so that he will have the fare to pay Charon, as for Palamedes, he can work his passage.

I stand and look out over the city toward the sea gleaming like beaten tin. The road home. The sun is well past the midday mark on yet another trek across the sky. Its heat feels good, reassuring. Tyndareus had talked of the blind optimism of flowers, it holds for men, too, or is the heart little more than a blind mule turning a pump handle?

I leave the wall and wander through the city streets where the admirably disciplined Achaeans have been overtaken by dementia. Frenzy glazes their eyes as they rape corpses and steal anything that shines. They leap from roofs and elbow each other aside to get at women. They are crazed, they bludgeon children as if they were rabid dogs. What a proud moment. We kings. We victors. We noble warriors blessed by the gods. Only Diomedes declines to indulge, he stands forlorn, slope-shouldered and brooding, sword dangling forgotten in his hand.

"Dio . . ."

He looks at me, eyes heavy with the weight of disappointment, worse, disenchantment. "There are no gods here, Odysseus. I've looked." As if it has all been a waste, he pitches his sword down, it clatters sparking against the stone, striking blue and gold chips of fire like a hammer on an anvil. We share the same thought: Hephaestus, lame god of blacksmiths. We exchange glances. Diomedes sneers at the sky. "Hephaestus . . ." Disgusted, he stalks off saying that he'll not fight a cripple.

Outside the gate the wind gusts dirt into my eyes. I turn away but can't avoid the wet coin smell of blood. Corpses lie heaped in drifts against the walls. Sinon, Dercynus, and Echion should be here, happy, embracing, running toward our ships, and of course Ajax. It is both a wonder and a humiliation to me that despite all of this I can still take solace in a new day, in the fact that the sun is shining, that at long last the Trojan War is finished, that Palamedes is dead, Agamemnon has his city, Menelaus his woman, and soon, very soon, in a month at most, I will be home.

The author of six novels, one collection of stories, and a book on India, **Grant Buday** has
travelled widely and now lives on a small island
with his wife and son.

Marquis Book Printing Inc.

Québec, Canada
2008